STAY TI

Who but a heartless monster like Brent Napier would callously turn a girl out of the only home she had? Linette thought bitterly. And, having turned her out, couldn't he be content with that? Why did he have to keep interfering in her personal affairs as well?

# STAY TILL MORNING

BY

## LILIAN PEAKE

MILLS & BOON LIMITED
15-16 BROOK'S MEWS
LONDON W1A 1DR

*First published 1982*
*Australian copyright 1982*
*Philippine copyright 1982*
*This edition 1982*

© Lilian Peake 1982

ISBN 0 263 73903 1

*Set in Monophoto Baskerville 10 on 10½ pt.*
*01-0882 · 61623*

*Made and printed in Great Britain by*
*Richard Clay (The Chaucer Press) Ltd,*
*Bungay, Suffolk*

# CHAPTER ONE

As soon as Linette saw her Uncle Godfrey climb out of his van, she knew there was something wrong. For some weeks she had had her suspicions, but had never questioned him directly. Nor was it the right time now, she reminded herself, with a customer waiting patiently for her to bring her mind back to her work.

Out of the corner of her eye she saw her uncle make for the front entrance of the cottage in which they lived. His shoulders were slightly bent, his step slow. Keeping her anxiety in check, Linette continued to serve the young housewife with the fruit and vegetable products of her uncle's flourishing garden.

As the young woman departed, Linette tried to concentrate on the display in front of her. The stall stood in a corner of the small front garden, which was a few yards distant from a busy road. The stall was decorated with brightly-coloured crêpe paper, but it did not need the decorations to attract custom.

The juicy blackcurrants, the raspberries and small baskets of late strawberries were sufficient to tug at the senses and purses of any passer-by. The vegetables held their own appeal, their fresh aroma stimulating the taste buds and promising appetising meals to come.

Her Uncle Godfrey appeared at the doorway. 'I've got something to tell you,' he announced, consulting his watch. 'But it'll keep until you've finished there.'

Linette nodded and abstractedly straightened a basket of strawberries, admiring their size and colour. She frowned at the leeks on display, although their condition was perfect. Then a flowering potted plant received the benefit of her anxious gaze.

'I had a feeling there was something wrong,' she told her uncle. 'You've been quiet lately, but I thought maybe

5

you were——' Even now, three years later, she felt it pained her uncle to talk about his loss.

'Thought I was still mourning your dear aunt's passing? I am, deep down, but it's not that.'

Another customer approached and her uncle disappeared. The 'customer' was a small boy standing on tiptoe and handing over his mother's list. Linette smiled, knowing the child well. He was almost five years old and a member of the morning play-group she ran to give the children's mothers a chance to go shopping, visiting or, as Linette told them, just be themselves.

Later, when the garden produce had been packed away, Linette sat with her uncle at the table. The meal was over. It had been eaten in a thoughtful silence. Linette had watched as her uncle had tackled the food she had cooked him. She doubted if he really knew what he had been eating.

His eyes had held again the hurt expression which, three years before, the loss of his wife, Amy, had given them. What had happened now to bring back the pain?

Eighteen months after her aunt had died, Linette had left her parents' home in the north of England and gone south to join her uncle in the Gloucestershire countryside. She had given up her office job, too, but that had been no sacrifice.

Ever since she could remember, she had longed to live in the country. The chance had arisen when her uncle had told his sister—Linette's mother—that he needed help, young, strong help with his small business.

He wanted someone who would do the work his wife had done, assisting him with the fruit bushes, the weeding and the cultivation. Most of all, he needed assistance with the selling of his produce. Linette had seized the chance to fulfil her dream and it was not long before she had gone to join her uncle in the country.

Without looking at her, Godfrey started speaking. 'For seven years now, I've been a tenant here, a good tenant. Paid my rent monthly, right on time.' He reached into an inside pocket. 'Yet all the thanks I get is this!' He threw a letter on to the table. 'Notice to quit.'

Linette was too horrified to speak.

'I know what you're thinking,' her uncle said. 'I've got an agreement with the owner.'

'Well, it's true,' Linette declared, her blue eyes fierce. 'Which means he can't do this to you. Legally, he's in the wrong.'

Godfrey was shaking his head. 'That's the worry. The agreement has lapsed. Every year, Mr Napier's solicitors have renewed it on the dot. This time I've been waiting weeks for them to renew it. I even telephoned them, but they hedged and quibbled. So I went to see them.'

Linette's bright eyes were expectant. 'What did they say?'

'Very little. The new owner intends to take up residence in the big house. Mr Brent "Industrialist" Napier was travelling the world on business. He's sold his house in London, and he wants this cottage for his mother. They couldn't contact him because he's left no definite address or itinerary. Or so they said.'

Linette had never known her uncle be so bitter.

'Industrialist? Is that what he is?'

'He's in the chemicals and pharmaceuticals business. Branching out now, I heard, into other fields. Worldwide company, one of the top men.' Godfrey's curled fist hit the table. 'I don't care how high and mighty he is, I'm not budging from my home and my garden!'

'If it makes you feel any better, Uncle,' Linette told him, 'I'm with you all the way. I'll fight him, tooth and claw if necessary!' Her eyes flashed with indignation.

'I doubt,' her uncle took her up, 'if you'll ever get near enough to the man to touch him, let alone bite and claw him!'

'I'll find a way,' Linette promised darkly. Somehow, she vowed, she would defend her uncle's right to remain in the cottage he loved.

The question was, did her uncle have any rights at all? Since no new agreement had been exchanged with the owner, presumably on that owner's directive, her reason told her 'no', but her sense of justice said, Yes, yes, he must have!

The cottage was built of gold-grey Cotswold stone. It must have stood, her uncle had estimated, for almost three centuries. Its roof was showing the weight of years, yet its three dormer windows, with miniature roofs of their own, stood proud and thrusting from it.

Over the entrance porch there was a small, gabled roof. The downstairs windows had been renovated and there were plants and shrubs around the base, one or two trained to climb to door height.

The building had about it a loved look. And so it should, Linette reasoned, since it had been so well cared for by her uncle and, when she had been there, her aunt.

The path to the door was cobbled and it was with care that, the following day, the small children were led over it by their parents. With a wide smile Linette welcomed the young play-group members. Three mornings a week they trotted in, and Linette was always sorry to see them go.

Later, she cleared the floor of the small back room where they had played. Toys went into cupboards, books on to shelves. Forgotten items were put aside for collection next time. Having cleaned the small blackboard on its trestle, she folded it away.

Her uncle came in as she straightened. He held a letter and his face was pale. He looked around. 'All gone?' Linette nodded. 'This came this morning.' He waved the letter. 'I thought I'd better tell you after the kiddies had left.'

Linette removed the protective apron she had been wearing, folding it with unnecessary care. What was coming now? she wondered with dread.

'They've managed to contact Mr Napier.' Godfrey's voice was tight, as if he was having trouble breathing. 'He says if we don't get out, they'll turn us out.'

'Forcibly?'

Her uncle nodded. 'Bailiffs.'

'When—when are they coming, Uncle?'

'Who knows? They won't tell us, will they?'

'Not yet, surely? I mean, all this has only just happened——'

Godfrey shook his head. 'It's been going on for some weeks. I didn't want to worry you. I thought I could fight it myself. I didn't count on him using the "dirty tricks department".'

'Using bailiffs, you mean?' Linette took a breath. 'What's he like, this man—this monster? What's he made of? I'd like to get at him . . .'

Godfrey's head was dismissive. 'You'd make not a jot of impression. Big business man, owns a large country house,' he indicated the mellowed, gabled mansion in the near distance, 'probably owns a flat in town, too. Behind him, there's his mother egging him on because she wants her greedy hands on this lovely—this beautiful——' His voice cracked.

'Little cottage,' Linette finished for him, and he nodded. 'Uncle Godfrey, surely even he would give us a final date——'

'He did, or rather the solicitors did. It was five weeks ago.' He looked a little sheepish.

'You didn't tell me? Uncle, how could you?'

'I'm the tenant. There was nothing you could do.'

Linette had to acknowledge the truth in her uncle's statement. He was, she felt, capable of fighting his own battles. Of medium height and agile, despite his near-white hair, his whole raison d'être was bound up in the small but flourishing plot of land adjoining the cottage. He would fight to keep it with every weapon he possessed. And I, she thought with a fiery loyalty, will only be a step behind.

Two mornings later she stood again at the front entrance of the cottage. One by one, she welcomed and counted the five small children who walked, with varying degrees of stability along the cobbled path. There was one child missing. Linette's arms were wide for each new arrival and the mothers' hands were easily slipped from small clutching fingers.

As Linette waved to the departing parents, her eye was caught by a sleek blue car which had drawn up at the opposite kerb. The driver—most certainly male—was regarding her with a penetrating, if inscrutable, gaze.

Linette's heart skipped with shock and puzzlement. What had she done to deserve such a look of censure—and from a stranger, too? Strong with the knowledge of her innocence of any 'crime', she threw back his look, wishing it was a missile which on impact would take that arrogant and censorious expression from his face.

The man remained unmoved by her anger. His dark brown hair was a little unruly, as if the breeze had ruffled it through the opened window. His head stayed high, his eyes piercing. With relief, she saw the arrival of the car which was about to deliver the missing member of the play-group.

It was a single-parent family who made its way towards her—father and small daughter. Again, Linette's arms spread wide, enclosing a hugging child. Linette's eyes lifted to those of the father. He was smiling down at her, but in his eyes was the faintest hint of despair. Linette knew the reason only too well.

How often had the man's four-year-old daughter, Jenny, whispered to her, 'My mummy hasn't come back yet.'

'Sorry we're late, Linette,' the father said, his harassed look retreating.

'But Leslie,' Linette joked, 'you always are.' She kissed the little girl's cheek. 'Tell your daddy I forgive him, Jenny.'

Obediently, the child repeated the words, then kissed her crouching father's cheek. Leslie straightened.

'I'm alone tonight, Linette.' His expression added, I'm alone every night. 'Would you join me for a meal? It would cheer me up a lot if you'd say "yes".'

Linette stood, pushing at her brown curling hair. The car with the coldly staring stranger had not moved. Her reason urged her to refuse the plaintive invitation, since she had no wish to become involved in a complex family problem, but something in the stranger's expression made her smile and accept.

The colour which suffused the father's cheeks told her of his delight. For some time he had been trying to coax her into a friendship closer than a mutual interest in his daughter's welfare. He waved to a now-impatient Jenny, who darted into the cottage to join her friends.

Leslie's car, Linette reflected, watching as it drew to a standstill outside her uncle's cottage, was small and un-pretentious. It was tailor-made to suit its owner's per-sonality—steady, stable and just a little stolid. Was it, perhaps, these qualities which had driven his young wife away? From the brief, confiding moments which had passed between them, Linette had learned that Jenny's mother had found greater excitement in the arms of another man.

Leslie took Linette to an expensive-looking hotel. When she saw the ivy-clad entrance porch, the hint of red and polished brass beyond the glass-paned doors, she turned to her companion.

'Are you sure?' she asked. His pained expression made her wish she hadn't.

The menu confirmed her suspicions of its expensiveness. She chose modestly and when questioned, assured her host that her tastes were simple.

The lighting cast a glow over tables and diners alike. Brassware decorated the walls, a wide high ledge just below the ceiling held Willow-Patterned dishes and examples of locally-made pottery.

During the meal, Leslie talked earnestly about his small daughter, saying again how much she missed her mother. The strain he was feeling as a result of hurrying from work to take over from the neighbour who looked after Jenny in his absence was, he confessed, beginning to tell.

Linette's heart went out to the man, but she could offer no more than words of comfort. Her eyes wandered over the other diners, admiring the women's dresses and wishing she could afford to buy better quality clothes.

One woman in particular caught her attention. Her fair hair was parted centrally and caught back into an attractive knot. Her earrings were large, their colour toning with the blue of her dress and jacket. Her movements were studied and elegant, and self-confidence added poise to her every gesture.

Her male companion, it seemed, was enraptured by her oval-shaped face . . . Her male companion? She had seen him before, hadn't she? He was the stranger in the car which, that morning, had parked for so long outside the cottage.

He was returning her stare. Linette's colour rose and she found that her fingers were pressing into her throat. Now she could see him, not only his eyes, which this time were narrowed, but the hard planes of his facial structure, his full mouth and stubborn jaw. The sight of him made an impact which winded her as painfully as if she had actually crashed into him.

He leaned back in his seat, his long legs crossed, and allowed his gaze to wander over her. Involuntarily, her hand tugged at her skirt. In a vain attempt to flatten the springing curls, she smoothed her hair. Until now she had not been conscious of her modest style of dress and her general air of artlessness.

With his lady companion as a measure, the man's judgment of her, Linette, would be dismissive and condemning. As if to confirm her belief, he straightened. With an elbow on the table, he gave his entire attention to the sophisticated woman seated across from him.

'Do you know that man?' Leslie's question jogged her back to his presence.

'Not really. I—well, I'm sure I've seen him before. There was a car across the road from the cottage this morning——'

'He was in the driving seat? I remember the car.' Leslie stole a covert glance. 'I think you're right.'

'He stared,' Linette complained,' he annoyed me.'

Leslie laughed. 'Don't let it worry you. He's probably just a tourist. They crowd the area in the summer, as you probably know by now.'

Linette's eyes crept round. 'He doesn't look like a tourist.'

Again, her eyes were ensnared by the man, by the perfect fit of his evening wear, the shoulders which thrust wide and challengingly, the thighs stretching tautly the fabric of his clothes. A tourist, she conceded, might if sufficiently affluent bother to bring in his suitcase such an outfit in which to entertain a special guest.

Yet no tourist would carry around with him so obtrusively the aura of the business world which swirled about the stranger. All the other holiday visitors she had seen looked about them wonderingly, relaxed and smiling.

The stranger appeared to sense her scrutiny and his head came round again. His handsome face contained eyes as hard as granite. They rebuked, giving stare for stare.

'Forget the man,' Leslie advised, and Linette detected a note of pleading.

'Sorry,' she murmured, suggesting more coffee. Leslie accepted and she poured, surprised to see the faint shake of her hand. Had Leslie noticed? Handing him his cup, she was satisfied that he had not.

'Am I boring you?' he questioned, and Linette reproached herself for her inattention to her host. It was all the fault of that stranger, she fumed. For some curious reason he had upset her, touched a mental nerve. She would forget the man's existence—even if it did present a threat.

The word had flashed through her mind, surprising her. A threat—to what? Her peace of mind? Her comparative inadequacy in the face of his guest's attractiveness? Yes, that was it, she decided, drawing a breath and answering Leslie's question with a decisive, 'Of course not. Er—let's talk about the weather!'

Leslie laughed.

'No,' Linette corrected, 'I can think of better subjects, things I can't discuss with my uncle. Sometimes he's so immersed in his work, or thoughts of it, he doesn't even hear when I talk to him.'

Leslie smiled. 'What subject, then? Books, politics?'

Linette shook her head. 'More human things, like—like how much I enjoy my three mornings with the children. How I try to pass on to them the kind of love my parents gave, and still give, to me.'

A frown creased Leslie's forehead, then it was gone. Had she touched on a nerve in him, making him wince? It seemed so as his voice shook a little as he repeated her word, 'Love. It was something I thought I shared with my wife.' His shoulders lifted and Linette noticed how loosely his jacket fitted him, as if he had gone thinner.

'Let's talk about books,' she exclaimed, and they laughed together.

Next morning, Linette arranged the produce from her uncle's garden with her usual pride and care. To her own annoyance, she found her eyes scanning the road for the sight of a car whose driver had caused her to toss and turn in her bed the night before. He had even, she remembered irritably, had the audacity to invade her dreams—all of which had somehow turned into nightmares.

As she was weighing the assorted baskets, making certain that everyone who bought from her uncle received the exact amount they paid for, the blue car slid into view. Cursing herself for her carelessness, she stooped down to pick up one by one the fruit she had spilled.

The dropped raspberries were so bruised and dusty, she could only discard them. Rubbing her hands on a cloth, she busied herself again, making an immense attempt to banish the car, and more especially its driver, from her mind. If, she reasoned, I've willed him here, why can't I will him away again?

It was easier thought than done. If only her heart would stop behaving like a pneumatic drill gone berserk, if only her breaths would come less shallowly, as if she were running, she might have been able to concentrate on making her willpower dance to her mind's tune.

He was slamming his car door, dodging the traffic and coming across. His bronze-coloured short-sleeved shirt was taut across his chest. The belt of his leisure-wear slacks rested just above his hips, revealing a leanness which told of a life of activity and physical exercise.

His eyes had not softened since last night, Linette observed, lifting her own to the amber of his. On the contrary, they seemed, if that were possible, to have hardened, although what was harder than granite, she asked herself.

The keenness of his gaze was evidence of an active intellectual life, too. Mr Superbrain himself, she dubbed him sarcastically, in an effort to get even with this stranger who had dodged in and out of her thoughts for the past twenty-four hours.

He stood on the other side of the display of garden produce. His scrutiny shifted from an inspection of her to an examination of the goods on offer.

'Do you buy from a wholesaler?' he enquired.

The question flustered her. Who was this man that he could ask such a question? She began to panic. Did he represent authority, was he a lawyer, had he any powers? Most important of all, should she call her uncle?

It was the thought of him that sparked off her belligerence. She did not care who he was—he would get only the truth from her! 'All my customers know they're buying my uncle's produce. It's freshly-pulled,' she touched the lettuces, 'and picked,' she nodded to the varied berries in their tiny baskets, 'from his garden.' Her hand gestured behind her and the stranger gazed his fill at the multiplicity of colours which filled the low-walled area.

He nodded, then turned his attention to the fruit, selecting a basket of strawberries. 'These look a little the worse for wear.'

'It's late in the season for them,' Linette answered, over-sharply. 'You're lucky to be able to buy any now. But my uncle's looked after them carefully.' Her eyes burned with restrained anger. 'He takes great care of everything he grows.'

'I'm sure he does,' the stranger drawled, and Linette's skin crawled at the cynical look in his eyes. 'You called it "his garden". Does that mean he owns the cottage to which the garden belongs?'

For some reason, Linette felt that the question was loaded. What was he trying to get her to say? It annoyed her that she had to tell this man 'no.'

She shook her head. 'He rents the place. He's been here for quite a few years. The garden's his pride and joy.' She held out the bag containing the strawberries. 'I help him with it in my spare time.'

'When you're not clasping small children to your bosom.' His eyes dropped to dwell on that part of her anatomy. The action was a slow calculated insult. He handed her some money and she thrust the change towards him. He stretched across and closed her fingers over her palm, trapping the coins. 'Keep it. You may need it one day.'

Fury erupted inside her. He was beginning to walk away, but she raised her arm and flung the coins after him. 'I hope I never see you again!' she cried.

He turned and saw the scattered money on the ground, then he dwelt with a sardonic smile on her angry colour.

'That,' he answered blandly, 'I cannot promise.'

His car engine roared as he drove away.


## CHAPTER TWO


LINETTE told her uncle about the incident. Even now, hours later, when the sun glowed golden and near to setting through the leafy lacework of the trees, the man still bothered her.

He dismissed the whole subject, sayng, 'It was probably you he was after. You're a pretty girl, although you may not know it. You shouldn't be here with me, really. You should be out in the world, enjoying yourself.'

He sounded so full of self-reproach that Linette rushed to reassure him. 'I'm twenty-three. I know my own mind now, Uncle Godfrey. I'm happy here.' She smiled. 'That's what matters, isn't it?'

Her uncle seemed pleased, but his pleasure did not set her mind at rest. 'It couldn't have been me, Uncle Godfrey,' she reflected. 'You see, last night Leslie took me to a very nice restaurant for a meal. That man was there, with a really attractive-looking woman. Well, attractive in a hard way, but then he's hard, too.'

'They should go well together,' her uncle observed dryly, moving to an armchair. 'Although it beats me how you seem to know so much about his character. You've only spoken to him once.'

'I've seen him three times. It may not seem much, but somehow, I know it in my bones——' She glanced at the tired form of her mother's brother. She couldn't say to him, that man has bad intentions towards us. Her uncle had not seemed to notice she had cut off in mid-sentence. His eyes were closed and she cleared the table quietly so as not to disturb his evening rest.

The curtains were pulled and the television was on when there was a hammering at the door. Linette hurried to answer it. To her relief, it was Leslie. Who else had I expected? she asked herself. All the same, Leslie seemed agitated.

Linette showed him to a chair. Her uncle had switched off the television set. 'There's nothing wrong with Jenny, is there?' Linette asked anxiously.

Leslie shook his head. 'I left the neighbour keeping an eye on her. No, it concerns you—and your uncle. Mr Barker,' Leslie urged forward, 'I was having a beer in the pub——' to Linette, 'I go there in the evenings sometimes for company—and I overheard two men talking. They're there most times when I go.'

Godfrey was straining forward, frowning and anxious.

'They said the bloke who owns your cottage is fed up with waiting. He's told his solicitors to use strong-arm methods to get you out. They only heard this evening, they said. There's a group of men coming in a day or two to put you out of here.'

'Bailiffs?' Linette barely whispered.

Godrey had gone pale, but he spoke fighting words. 'I'll be ready for 'em,' he promised. 'They'll not get me, nor my niece, to put a foot outside this cottage!'

'But, Uncle,' her fingers made indentations in her cheek, 'there's only two of us. I'm game to fight, but you——'

'I'm not past it, lass. I may be in my late fifties, but I'm hale and hearty, thank goodness.'

'I'll join you,' Leslie offered.

'No, no, lad, you've got your job to go to. Don't you lose any pay for us.'

'Linette?' Leslie asked.

'No, Leslie. You might get hurt, and you're all Jenny's got. Thanks for offering, though.' She squeezed his hand and he coloured with a faint pleasure.

Leslie went away reluctantly, having drunk the coffee Linette had made. 'Take care, Linette,' he pleaded. 'And you, Mr Barker.'

'We'll take care, lad. Of ourselves and the cottage, too.'

Linette suspected that her uncle, like herself, did not sleep well that night. The bad dreams recurred, but there was not a single strong-armed, hard-hearted man in sight. Only one person kept intruding—the cold-eyed stranger who had watched her, bought from her, insulted her and watched her again as she had dined with Leslie.

When the children arrived after breakfast, she promised herself that not one sign of her inner fears would be communicated to them. Her uncle had spoken little through his entire meal, and she suspected that he, in his turn, was endeavouring to hide his anxiety.

Leslie, last as usual, brought a dancing Jenny to the door. 'Here's my phone number at work,' he said, handing Linette a scribbled-on scrap of paper. 'Ring that extension and I'll be on the other end. Don't hesitate, will you?'

'You're very kind,' Linette told him, moved by his concern. 'I'm really grateful, Leslie.' Spontaneously she reached up to kiss his cheek.

The sound of a vehicle gaining speed made them both turn. A large blue car disappeared into the distance.

'That man—he was watching again!' Linette said furiously. 'What is he, some secret agent?'

Leslie shook his head, nonplussed. He glanced at the time, said he must go and waved himself away. The children behaved boisterously that morning. Linette wondered if her worries were showing up in another way—an inability to control them as firmly as she usually did.

All the same, their bright-eyed mischief kept her mind constantly on them, and only now and then did her attention stray. On one occasion, she found herself actually staring out of the window which overlooked the street. At once she reproached herself. Was she actually *looking* for the man?

All morning they waited. Linette could almost feel her uncle's tension as they met over lunch. Yet he stolidly stoked himself with food, as if he were taking in all the energy he could absorb while he could get it. Did he, Linette wondered, envisage a time when their supplies might run out? She shivered at the thought and at what that thought implied.

Leslie, when collecting his daughter, had commented on Linette's serenity in view of the rumour he had heard.

'You might think I'm calm,' she answered, 'but inside I'm twisted into knots. If I ever meet the man responsible . . .'

Leslie had shaken his head and escorted a still-dancing daughter to his car.

Linette felt more relaxed next morning after a surprisingly restful night. Her Uncle Godfrey also seemed more serene. She wondered if, like herself, he had persuaded himself to believe that the worst would never happen and that the owner had, sensibly, given up the fight to obtain possession of the cottage for his mother.

Godfrey went as usual into the garden, workmanlike in his old clothes. Linette set up the stall and arranged the display of fruits and vegetables. Customers came and went, remarking on the bright sunshine and how its warmth made everyone feel better-tempered.

A dark red van drew up a short distance down the road. An alarm buzzed in Linette's head, but when she saw the man who slammed the van door and walked towards her, she smiled with relief. He stopped in front of the stall.

' 'Morning, Mr Ellington,' Linette greeted him. 'Lovely day.' She indicated the fruit. 'All fresh from Uncle Godfrey's garden.'

'I know they are, miss.' The man's blank expression puzzled her. He went on, 'But it's not this I'm interested in. Is your uncle about? I'd like a word.' His tone of voice was so sharp the alarm buzzed again.

'I'll call him,' she said, and ran to search for her uncle in the garden. He was half hidden behind the sticks and twisting stalks and leaves of the runner beans. 'Mr Ellington, Uncle. Says he wants to see you. There, over by the stall.'

He was on his way and she had no time to tell him of her apprehension.

' 'Morning, Tom,' Godfrey greeted the newcomer. 'What can I do for you?'

'Get out of this cottage, Godfrey. That's what you can do for me.'

Godfrey's face did not lose its smile. Only his eyes changed, becoming wary. He shook his head slowly. 'Not even for you, Tom, could I do that. Linette and me, we're staying right here, Tom.' He lifted his head and looked into the distance. 'It doesn't matter how many of the lads you bring with you, either. You're not getting us out.'

Linette followed her uncle's eyes. Four men were making their slow way along the street, spreading out across the pavement. She recognised them all. They stood in a half-circle around Tom Ellington, waiting,

' 'Morning, Jack, Johnny . . .' Godfrey named them all.
One of them was around Linette's age. He had once asked
her out. His eyes looked sad as they dwelt on her.

'Sorry, Lin,' he said, 'but—well, I need the money, see?
We're being well paid.' This to Godfrey.

'I bet you are,' Linette put in bitterly. 'By the wonderful
Mr Brent Napier, no doubt. If I could lay my hands on
that Mr Napier!'

'Turning friend against friend,' her uncle added. 'How
could he? And how could you, Tom? How many years
have I known you?'

'Look, Godfrey, I don't like doing this sort of thing. The
wife said I wasn't to, but the money—we need it to buy
things.' The other men nodded vigorously.

'I need money, too, Tom,' Godfrey told him, 'the money
all my hard work brings in.' He nodded to the stall,
motioned towards the garden. 'For years I've worked on
that bit of land. It's a treat to grow things on it now. I
couldn't leave it, Tom. You're a farmer. I know you
understand.'

'Look, Godfrey——' He took a breath, trying to regain
his belligerence, then let out his breath in a sigh. 'I can't
do it, lads. Come on, I need a drink, but it's a bit too early.
Pubs aren't open yet.'

'Come in, Tom, Johnny, all of you. Have a glass of my
stuff. I brew my own beer, you know that.'

Her uncle was inviting them into his cottage? Was it
wise? 'Uncle——?'

'We won't harm him, miss,' Tom allayed her fears. 'Nor
your things. We'll forget the money. Agreed, boys?'

The men nodded, shaking Godfrey's hand. Johnny had
a special smile for Linette as he disappeared into the cottage. She sighed with relief, thinking, Point to us, Mr
Brent Napier. You can't get us out that way. My uncle's
too popular among all his friends and neighbours.

The sky was cloudy when the children arrived next
morning, but that did not dull their spirits. They were

spraying water over her from an old detergent container when she heard her uncle shouting. He was calling her name and she ran to the door of the room, telling the children to be quiet.

'Stay there,' she instructed, then raced outside. A van stood by the kerb, larger this time. Against it stood five burly men. Linette had never seen them before. Her face drained of colour, her heart started pounding.

The man Brent Napier had been clever. These were complete strangers, from the nearby town, she guessed. There were no links of friendship or good-neighbourliness to soften their attitudes. These men were the real thing. To them, ejecting people from their homes was their work— work they carried out without heart, without scruple.

Linette dashed back into the house and dialled Leslie's number, which she had memorised. The children had begun to whimper and Leslie could hear them as she whispered, 'They're here, Leslie. They're going to evict us.'

'I'll be right there. Five minutes, that's all.'

Linette had no time to offer him her thanks. 'Stay there,' she told the children again, and rejoined her uncle. The five men, in a row, had moved through the garden gate and were spread in a line against the low wall, thus cutting off the only escape route.

'Uncle,' she said, 'Uncle . . . what do we do?' No use whispering. The men were experienced, knew all the weaknesses of their victims, knew how their own size and tactics intimidated.

'What do we do, lass?' Her uncle's voice rang out proudly. 'We stay, that's what we do.'

The row of men came a step nearer. They seemed to be concentrating on her uncle. Linette ran to his side, clinging to his arm. 'Leave my uncle alone, you bullies!' she cried.

'Now that's no way to speak to nice men like us, miss,' one of the younger men said. His eyes appreciated her freshness, but held no insolence. 'We don't want to hurt the old man, nor you, miss. So, if you'll come quietly . . .'

She had to play for time until Leslie arrived. 'Uncle

Godfrey's not old,' she fenced. 'His heart's in that cottage, his memories——'

'Don't give us that, miss,' another man said long-sufferingly, 'we've heard it all before.'

Leslie came with a screech of brakes. He used surprise to get him through the row of solidly-constructed men and joined Linette. She looked at him gratefully. 'Leslie, the kids—they're in there alone.'

'He your husband, miss?'

'No,' she told the man. 'I run a play-group. Six children are in there. If you dare harm them——'

The men exchanged glances. Linette's eyes were drawn to the road. A man had emerged from a large blue car. He was approaching. One man whispered a message to the other who seemed to be the leader. He looked round.

'Slow business, Mr Napier, but we'll do the job, don't you worry. We're biding our time.'

A milkman passed, staring horrified from his electric vehicle, then went on his way.

Linette looked at the tall, lean man standing outside the gate. 'That's Mr Napier, Mr Brent Napier?' Her breath came quickly and she shouted, 'I'm going to tear him to pieces!'

'Linette,' her uncle cautioned agitatedly, 'don't touch the man, do you hear?' She ignored the advice.

Even as she made to dive through the lines, one of the men caught her. Such was her frenzy, she struggled free and dashed through the gate. Brent Napier had not moved. He stood, hands on hips, legs apart, face expressionless, waiting.

Tugging at his sleeves, catching at his jacket, she cried, 'Brute, inhuman monster! Haven't you any feelings? It's our home you're taking away from us!'

His hands came up to catch her wrists, stilling her flailing arms. He jerked her against him, pulling down her hands behind her back and holding them in one of his. He stared into her upturned face, filled with hatred of him and a raging anger.

He was hurting her, but she would not tell him. 'Leslie!' she shouted and he appeared at the cottage door. 'Look after the children. Those men are savages! Under orders from *this* man, you don't know what they'll do to them.'

'We won't harm the kiddies, miss,' one of the men called. 'It's your uncle we're after. And you.'

In vain she twisted and turned in Brent Napier's hold. 'Don't you touch my uncle! He's not young any more. It doesn't matter about me . . .'

'Such self-sacrifice, Miss Kemp,' Brent Napier drawled. 'Do you think it will touch my heart?'

'You haven't got a heart!'

'What'll we do, Mr Napier?' the leader of the men wanted to know.

'Start on the downstairs furniture,' he called. 'Put it on the pavement.'

'The children are downstairs,' she said, horrified.

'Cancel that decision,' Brent told them. 'Upstairs, first.' The men had not moved. Brent Napier urged her closer. She could feel the imprint of his thighs against her. 'Are you going to co-operate? I'll give you one minute before I say "go".'

Her uncle's voice said sharply, 'Even if she does, I refuse.'

'I won't, Uncle,' she reassured him, gritting her teeth as the binding hands tightened on her wrists. Her pulses were leaping at the touch of this man who held her prisoner and she hated her body for letting her down. How could it allow a man she abhorred to stir her so deeply?

'I could get you,' his voice remarked softly, 'for assault as well as slander.'

There was an argument behind her and Brent's narrowed eyes lifted over her head. 'Your boy-friend's being difficult. He's doing his puny best to prevent the bailiffs from carrying out their job.'

Linette strained to gaze over her shoulder. Suddenly, her wrists were free.

'Warn him, Miss Kemp,' the dangerously quiet voice

advised. 'Tell him he could be in trouble with the law if he continues.'

Leslie's arms were spread wide, attempting to prevent two men from carrying out a chest of drawers. 'Leslie,' she urged, her voice thick, 'please don't get involved. Just look after the kids, especially Jenny.'

'Jenny's your daughter, Miss Kemp?' Brent Napier grated.

She rounded on him. 'No, she is not! She's Leslie's. Anyway, what business is it of yours?'

A car drew up and one of the mothers got out. 'Linette, what's going on?' she asked. 'Oh, my goodness!' as she took in the situation. 'I must get my Diane out of this.'

'How did you know, Caroline?' Linette enquired.

'The milkman saw what was happening. He's going round telling everyone. It's spread like the plague.' Another car braked. 'Here's Millicent. And Jill's with her.'

One by one, the mothers took away their children. Some were crying. Despairingly, but hiding it, Linette watched. Jenny ran to Linette, flinging her arms around her hips. Linette crouched down, hugging her, wishing she could allow her own tears to come. 'See you on Monday, pet,' she soothed. 'We'll still be here, I promise you that.'

'Don't make promises you won't be able to keep, Miss Kemp.'

The curt warning incensed her and she faced her tormentor.

'You'll have to—to *kill* my uncle and me before you get us out of that cottage!'

'I doubt if it will really prove necessary to go to those lengths,' he replied blandly.

The children had gone. Leslie lingered, but Jenny tugged at his hand. 'Please go, Leslie,' Linette whispered. 'There's nothing you can do now.'

With reluctance, he drove his daughter away. There was an uncertain silence. The men had deposited the chest of drawers outside the gate. It looked forlorn, shabby, but much loved.

'It's mine,' Linette whispered. 'They must have started on my room.' She remembered the small ornaments displayed on shelves, her clothes carefully laundered. Catching at a sob, she walked slowly to join her uncle as he stood beside the entrance door.

Together, they faced the intruders and beyond them, their landlord.

'Well, Mr Barker,' Brent Napier asked, 'are you now willing to co-operate?'

'I've been a good tenant, Mr Napier,' Godfrey's voice rang out. 'Paid my rent on time every month, kept the place in good repair and decoration. Put my heart and soul into that garden. I live a clean and decent life. What more could you want from a tenant?'

There must have been a signal, because the men resumed their activities.

Linette's arm went across her uncle's shoulders. Despite his apparent calmness, she discovered he was shaking.

'I have no criticism of you, Mr Barker. I merely want the cottage empty.'

There was a rattle as though china and glass was slipping and sliding. The men appeared with a set of white display shelves. As they lowered it to the grass, some of the ornaments fell and crashed to pieces.

Linette hid her gasp behind her hand. Her eyes stared her hatred at the man who had ordered the ransacking of the cottage. 'They're broken,' she choked. 'My precious things!' She gazed at the pieces then raised her eyes. 'Why, you miserable b——'

'Don't say it, pet,' her uncle warned. His head turned swiftly, as if an extra sense had told him something, and Linette followed his gasp. One of the men was grasping handfuls of plants and pulling them from the ground.

Her uncle started running. 'You swine!' he shouted. 'Leave my garden alone!' He stopped, doubled up, his anger having got the better of his body.

Linette dived again, through the gate to the man outside.

'I hate you, I hate you!' she screamed. 'Call them off! It's my uncle's most prized possession, that garden.' Her fists were all over him, frantic fingers pulled at his hair.

Again, his hands found her wrists, wrenching them away from him. He jerked her so hard against him, her body banged his. Her head was thrown back, revealing her storm-ridden eyes. They met twin icebergs which chilled her to her bones. There was no way of escaping their power, their ability to withstand and destroy whatever came into contact with them.

She felt her limbs loosen, her body sag. Collapsing against him, she knew she was their victim. 'You've won, Mr Napier,' she sobbed against the wall of his chest. 'You've crushed us. My uncle and I—we'll go quietly.' Her head lifted, but her hands were still in Brent Napier's grasp so she could not wipe away her tears. 'Won't we, Uncle?' she said half over her shoulder.

The grasping hands thrust her away, and she swung her head to look at the face of the man who had released her. A new knowledge leapt to life inside her, but she had no code with which to unravel its meaning. His eyes caught fire from the flare in hers, then the fire was dowsed as the customary coldness returned.

'Leave it, men,' Brent Napier ordered curtly. 'Take back the things you've brought out.'

Linette stood at her uncle's side. In the past half-hour, he seemed to have aged ten years. They watched as Brent Napier came through the gate. He bent, retrieved a handful of broken china and walked across to Linette.

He took her hand, opened the palm and placed the pieces of it, closing her fingers over them. His face told her nothing. What had hers told him? He was so gentle she could have cried. As he walked away, she stared at the contents of her hand. She could have sworn, for a fleeting moment, that they had arranged themselves into the shape of her heart.

'Uncle Godfrey,' Linette attracted her uncle's brooding

attention as he sat, elbows on the table, 'what are we going to do?' The midday meal was over.

Godfrey sighed, shaking his head. 'The law's on his side. We could consult a solicitor, go to court, get a month or two's postponement of the inevitable. But we'd still have to get out, eventually.'

Linette's thoughts returned, as they had continually since his departure, to their tormentor and landlord, Brent Napier. It was impossible to get out of her mind the flare of feeling the touch of him against her had provoked. She tried constantly to analyse the sensations he had aroused.

It went against all rational thought to feel anything but intense dislike for such a man. Maybe that was the form such violent hatred took—an uprush of sensations which involved every part of one's being. If it was hatred, she mused, wouldn't she have wanted to hit out and run? Yet she had had no inclination to break away, to dust the touch of him from her hands and body.

Instead, she had been like a pin clinging to a magnet. The longer the contact had lasted, the more magnetised she had grown—until the moment when she had been forced to prise herself away.

She pressed her head between her hands, as if wanting to squeeze from it such treacherous thoughts. Her uncle's flat questioning ended her introspection.

'Did they do any damage, Linette?'

'Apart from putting a bump or two into the wood of the chest of drawers and smashing some of my china ornaments, no.'

Aware that there was some humour in her answer, she was not surprised when her uncle commented dryly, 'That's surely enough to be going on with?' A smile flickered across his face, immediately dying away.

'Oh, Uncle!' Her deep despair erupted unawares, and she hid her face in her hands.

'Now now, lass.' Godfrey's arm extended vaguely towards her. 'We'll find a way.'

Even if it's down the garden path and through the

garden gate, watching it swing irrevocably shut behind them. The thought came and went, unspoken.

That afternoon, Linette cleaned through the cottage. Her actions were so vigorous it was as though she felt a compulsion to rid the place of all traces of the morning's intruders. The furniture shone, the floorboards gleamed, the golden reflections from the wall brasses dazzled.

Later, she joined her uncle in the garden. Were his movements really slower than usual? she wondered. He caught her contemplative glance. It must have acted as a challenge, for he threw the fork into the soft soil, placed his booted foot on it and dug for all he was worth. Linette smiled and was thankful.

Over the weekend, she removed all traces of the broken pottery and china from the front garden. As she held them in her hand, she recalled how Brent Napier had closed her fingers over the pieces he had retreived.

Her mind remembered also the similar gesture he had made after telling her to 'keep the change'.

'You may need it one day', he'd said. He must have had the bailiffs in mind even then. Resentment swirled, blurring her vision. Deliberately, she conjured up the image of his face. It was no difficult feat, since it was happening all the time.

I'll use it as a mental dartboard, she told herself, only to discover that imaginary darts left no mark. There was no way in which she could score against him. What dismayed her most of all was the fact that she had no real desire to do so.

Monday morning found her looking forward eagerly to the children's arrival. I told them we'd still be here, she thought triumphantly, and we are! Until they arrived, she busied herself with arranging displays of flowers in every room. Deep inside her, there persisted the wish to keep celebrating. He didn't get us out, she thought, over and over again. He failed, we won!

Returning to the present, she frowned. It was ten minutes past the time at which the children were due to arrive. The telephone rang and she rushed to answer.

'Jill!' she exclaimed. 'I was wondering what had——'
She listened. 'You won't be bringing her? Not well? Sorry
to hear it. Never mind, Wednesday . . .'

Linette replaced the receiver slowly. Maybe, Jill had
said. It rang again, vibrating under her hand. 'Caroline?'
Linette's fingers gripped the yellow metal. 'Diane's not
coming? Not well? Sorry about that. See her Wed——'

'Not Wednesday, Linette,' Caroline interrupted. 'I think
I'd better tell you—on behalf of the others . . . We're
worried, you see. After what happened on Friday—well,
you might be there now, but——' the words came in a
rush, 'it could all happen again, couldn't it? It upset the
little ones——'

'I do understand,' Linette responded tautly. 'It won't
happen again, I'm certain it won't, but——'

'But it just might, mightn't it, and we don't want to take
any chances. You do see our point of view, Linette, don't
you?'

'I see it, Caroline, I see it only too well.' She couldn't
just put the phone down . . . 'Maybe,' she added, 'when
the dust has settled, I can contact you again?'

'Most certainly,' Caroline replied, too heartily. 'Oh,
and—thanks for all you've done, Lin. We've really
appreciated it.'

'Don't mention it,' Linette found herself saying. 'I've
enjoyed every single minute.'

There was a click in her ear. She stood, holding the
receiver, staring at nothing. Where was her happy feeling
now? He might have left them in peace for the moment,
but he had stolen from her something very precious. Happy
hours with the children, their warmth, their laughter . . .
Now it had all gone, smashed to fragments as surely as her
miniature ornaments. And this time she could not even
pick up the pieces.

'Linette?' Leslie stood there, holding Jenny's hand.
'Sorry we're late, but——'

Linette shook her head. 'The play-group doesn't exist

any more. That man—that man, it's all his fault.' She hid her face and turned away, hiding the smarting tears.

'Jenny, love,' she heard Leslie say, 'go and talk to Uncle Godfrey. He's there, in the garden.' Jenny ran away. Leslie's arm went round Linette's shoulders and he led her into the cottage.

There, in the deserted room which should, by now, have been ringing with the voices of the children, she found Leslie's comforting shoulder and wept her unhappiness out. Leslie did not speak. He stroked her hair and Linette sensed his feeling of inadequacy in dealing with the situation.

'Something wrong?' The sharp question came from the door.

Linette swung away from Leslie's support to face the newcomer. With the back of her hand she rubbed at her damp cheeks. She held her head up and flung at the speaker, 'There's everything wrong, and you're to blame, Mr Napier!'

'You're still here,' was the terse reply, 'so what catastrophe has overtaken you now?'

The veiled sarcasm scratched at her temper like barbed wire. 'So you've given us a temporary reprieve. How very thoughtful of you! If you really want to know, all the mothers have taken fright and the play-group's ended. They don't want their children to witness another scene like the one the other day. I can't say I blame them.'

'If you and your uncle co-operate, you have my word that scene, as you call it, won't happen again.'

'If we—*if we co-operate*? You mean if we walk out quietly——'

'Daddy?' Jenny was at the door, gazing large-eyed from Linette to the visitor.

Leslie glanced questioningly at Linette. 'Shall I take her home?'

'You can leave her, if you like,' Linette offered. 'I'll look after her——'

'The neighbour won't mind having her,' Leslie assured.

'After all, Jenny's got to get used to the idea of no more play-group.'

Jenny started wailing. 'Why, Daddy, why?' She clung to his hand. 'I want to come and see Linette and all my friends.'

Leslie picked up his daughter. ' 'Bye, Linette,' he called over his shoulder. A quick glance at Brent Napier, then, 'Good luck, Lin. I'll see you some time.'

After a few moments' silence, Linette asked, steadying her voice, 'What is this "co-operation" you want from us, Mr Napier? The old, old story—the sacrifice of the tenant's niece on the altar of the landlord's lustful desires?'

Brent Napier's smile reflected deep amusement. He put to one side the executive case he was carrying. 'Would that be so terrible, Miss Kemp? No woman these days surely approaches her mid-twenties, as I judge you're doing, without some knowledge and experience of a man's sensual needs?'

She vowed she would not reply to his insolent question, not even in response to his openly appreciative and very male examination of her shape and femininity. Her straining pink button-up blouse and snugly-fitting deep blue corduroy slacks did not seem to diminish her physical attractiveness in his eyes. Yet Linette, remembering his woman companion at the restaurant to which Leslie had taken her, found herself wishing she had dressed less casually.

Why should I want to please this man? she asked herself with annoyance. The fact remained that she did, that she found him attractive and wanted again to feel the strength of him holding her, not this time springing from anger, but from a much more pleasing source.

Her silence seemed to amuse him. Was there *nothing* about her, she wondered fretfully, that didn't arouse his mockery?

Long-fingered hands slipped into his pockets. The action tautened the fabric as it encased his lean thighs, emphasised the hard-boned hips. The open-necked shirt gave a glimpse of dark hair, the rolled-up sleeves revealed a similarly-coloured layer of fine hairs around which, at the wrist, his gold watch was clasped.

His eyes were laughing as he asked, 'Am I acceptable in your eyes as a male member of the human race, Miss Kemp? You may not know it, but you've been looking at me as if I were the devil in disguise.'

Colour crept into her face, but she answered with spirit, 'Just summing up the opposition, Mr Napier. Getting to know you, the enemy——'

He was confronting her in two strides. She felt the now-familiar grip of him on her arms. Yes, there was that latent strength which, only moments ago, had drifted dreamlike into her mind. 'Getting to *know* me, Miss Kemp? Let me demonstrate a better way of doing that than by looking.' He pulled her to him and she went, she could not stop herself. 'By touch, Miss Kemp, by physical contact.'

The glittering amber eyes that stared into hers nudged her into awareness that there were two choices ahead of her—red for danger, or green for 'go'. Red—for anger, not danger—prevailed and she gathered her strength to struggle. She couldn't allow any intimacy between herself and this man, even in the form of a fleeting kiss.

He easily stilled her twists and turns and she found herself even closer. His breath fanned her skin and she saw the jutting fullness of his lips. They descended on hers, holding them captive. Her hands gripped his upper arms and she felt their muscled hardness.

Momentarily his head lifted, giving her time to gasp one word—'No!' Then his mouth was back and this time his arms were round her. He drew her fully against him and she 'knew' him indeed, minutely, arousingly, fitting into the angles and the lean planes of him.

Then he put her from him and a kind of humiliation washed over her. 'So it's the old feudal story, after all, is it, Mr Napier?' she challenged, cursing the give-away heat that warmed her cheeks.

'I only wish it were, Miss Kemp,' he said levelly, 'then

I'd have had you forcibly brought to my bed the day you physically assaulted me. In handing out your punishment, I'd have made sure there was no mercy, no holds barred. Now,' he rolled down his sleeves, buttoning them, 'I'd like to get around to talking about the reason I came.'

If it had been his intention to cut her down to size, she thought, he'd certainly succeeded. As if *she* had been the one to initiate that kiss . .

'My mother would like to see over the cottage,' he went on. 'When is the best time for her to come?'

'Mornings, Mr Napier,' Linette answered in as business-like a way as she could manage. 'Any time she likes.'

'Good.'

'Is that the co-operation you were asking for, Mr Napier?' she enquired, her tone sugar-sweet.

'No. Since your uncle is the legal tenant, I wish to speak to him.'

Linette's ego shrank a little more. Simultaneously, her resentment grew. He was right, of course, but did he need to remind her of the fact so brusquely?

'He's busy in the garden. I'll get him.'

He nodded and proceeded to wander about, looking up at the ceiling, inspecting the state of the walls.

Pausing at the door, Linette declared, 'My uncle's kept the building in first-class condition. He's treated it for every possible architectural affliction known to man. I can assure you it's completely suitable for a female member of your family to occupy.'

In a stride, he was facing her. His fists clenched in his pockets, his teeth gritted. 'One day, Miss Kemp, your impudence will try my tolerance too far!'

Her resolve to stand up to him faltered just a little, but she braved his anger, saying, 'If you analyse what I've just said, Mr Napier, you'll realise I wasn't being impudent, just factual.'

Her attempt to clear herself seemed to exasperate him even more, but he contained his anger. 'Will you now ask your uncle if he can spare a few minutes to see me?'

Linette went outside and found her uncle approaching. 'Isn't that Mr Napier's car over there?' he asked, brushing his clothes with his hands.

'He wants to see you, Uncle Godfrey. Mrs Napier, his mother, would like to see the place. I said she could come any time.'

Godfrey entered the cottage, stamping his boots on the mat. 'She can come,' he grunted, 'but it doesn't mean she can stay. Where is he?'

'In the living-room, Uncle. He—he wants our co-operation.'

'Does he, indeed?' Godfrey growled, opening the door. 'If it's anything to do with moving out, he can want.' Brent Napier eyed Godfrey steadily. 'You won't get me moving from here, Mr Napier,' Godfrey told him. 'You can send the bailiffs, you can put me in prison, but you won't get me leaving this place on my own two feet.'

'I've a proposition to make to you, Mr Barker.'

Godfrey eased himself into a chair. 'I make no apology for my clothes, Mr Napier,' he commented. 'I'm a working man. I'm busy, too. I've no time to think about proposi-tions. Sit down, will you? Linette, I could do with a nice cup of tea.' He looked round. 'Where's the kiddies?' Linette explained. 'Their mothers are afraid to bring them, eh? That's something else you've done, Mr Napier. My niece loved having those children here. She'll miss them.'

'I get the feeling,' Brent remarked, finding a chair, 'I'm not welcome in your house, Mr Barker.'

'You're welcome any time as a guest.'

'Your meaning, Mr Barker, comes over loud and clear.' Brent Napier rose, thrust hands into pockets and wandered about. 'Miss Kemp,' as Linette turned to go, 'I should like coffee, if that's possible?'

Linette made tea for her uncle and coffee for herself and their guest. As she worked, she heard the rumble of voices. It did not seem to be a friendly discussion, but how could it be? she asked herself with a tinge of regret.

A tenant arguing his case for continuing possession with

a landlord determined to evict him was hardly a subject to give rise to cordiality and laughter. As she carried in the tray, her uncle was shaking his head. There was a wary silence as Linette distributed the contents of the tray.

'I poured it out in the kitchen, Mr Napier,' she commented, handing him his coffee. 'I hope you don't mind my lack of social graces in the circumstances.'

His expression, which had been severe, changed to irony as an eyebrow lifted at her muted sarcasm. He said softly, so that he could barely be heard over the clanging of Godfrey's stirring spoon, 'Having done battle with my tenant, I'm quite willing to take on his sub-tenant, too. Especially as it's the girl whose kiss I found so satisfying twenty minutes ago.'

Which puts me in my place, Linette thought, hoping that the poison in her look would reach him. From his smile, however, it seemed that he had already applied the antidote. She returned to her seat and drank some coffee.

'I won't do it,' her uncle declared, motioning towards the shining polished oak table.

'Won't do what, Uncle Godfrey?' Linette turned and saw a pile of black and white photographs.

'Move to that place.'

Linette asked, 'May I?' Brent Napier nodded. Scooping up the photographs, she studied them one by one.

'Look at them hard, Lin,' her uncle growled. 'Those are pictures of the cottage Mr Napier's offering us in exchange for this.'

Linette studied the different aspects of the tumbledown building. There were bare rafters, split floorboards and a sagging roof. She looked up, startled. 'But this isn't even a complete building!'

'It's a ramshackle, dilapidated, rotting old shed!' her uncle exclaimed, indignation reddening his cheeks. 'You'd only have to breathe on it to bring it down round your feet.'

'What do you expect my uncle to do, Mr Kemp?' Linette asked. 'Roll up his sleeves and——'

Brent Napier reached for his case, opened the lid and said, 'Look at these, Miss Kemp.'

He handed her a pile of colour photographs. Linette gasped. 'This, surely, isn't——? It is, Uncle, it is! Look,' she crouched beside him, 'renovated, rebuilt.' She seized a black and white photograph in one hand and flourished a colour picture in the other. 'Isn't it beautiful, now? Mr Napier, why didn't you show us——?' She paused, thrust the photographs on to her uncle's lap and straightened.

Her uncle studied the pictures, saying nothing. Silence from him often signalled a positive reaction, Linette knew, but she could not prevent herself from saying,

'You were clever, weren't you, Mr Napier? The "before and after" technique rarely fails, does it? And to show them to me first, making *me* act as the sales promoter . . .' She trailed to a stop at the sight of the darkened eyes, the thrusting jaw.

Yes, her accusations had been the final grain of sand to tip her uncle's finely balanced judgment. Godfrey pushed them aside. 'Like an over-made-up woman,' he snorted. 'Keep your painted, rebuilt cottage with all its cosmetic surgery. I'm staying right here, Mr Napier.'

Godfrey stood up, his slight form rigid, immovable, as if he were himself part of the very foundations and ages-old structure of his home.

Linette gathered the scattered photographs, thrust open the visitor's case and put them in, Rising, her face flushed with effort and remorse, she held out the case to its owner. Her wide blue eyes told him, 'I'm sorry, I'm sorry', but the dark look he shot at her as he accepted the case held no forgiveness at all.

At the door he said, 'My mother will call some time.' His hand came out. 'Mr Barker.' Godfrey, confused by the apparently friendly gesture, responded, putting his rough hand into the proffered one. 'Miss Kemp.' A terse nod came Linette's way, but an inexplicable trembling of her lips prevented her from framing a word in reply.

It was Linette's 'market' morning, as she liked to think of her fruit and vegetable-laden stall. The sun caught at the colours, enhancing them, bringing out the sweet, appetite-arousing smells of the fresh-picked produce.

A man leaned over the stone wall dividing Godfrey's flower garden from the road, alongside which it stretched, perfuming the air. The vegetable-growing area was to the rear of the cottage.

The main road was busy, mostly with local traffic. 'If it were one of those modern speedways,' Godfrey had often said, which was the name he gave to motorways, 'I'd have packed up and gone long ago.'

'Bad business the other day, Godfrey,' the man was saying, tapping his empty pipe on the wall.

Godfrey grunted.

'Heard the great man wanted your place for his mother.' Another grunt from Godfrey. 'Should've thought it was beneath the great lady's dignity to live in a humble cottage.'

'There's nothing humble about my cottage, Henry.'

'Didn't mean it that way, Godfrey,' Henry answered placidly.

Godfrey continued digging. Linette smiled to herself at the slow pace of the conversation. At last her uncle offered,

'Probably in her late sixties if she's a day. Fussy old bag, I don't doubt.'

'I'd have thought,' Henry went on, after a while, 'she'd have wanted to live in the big house. Much grander than this.'

'Probably wanted a place of her own. You know, "olde worlde", fill it with antiques, mustn't dirty the best Wilton carpet and all that.'

Henry nodded, pocketed his pipe and wandered towards the stall. As he stood inspecting the goods, a mother and small child approached. Behind her came a middle-aged woman. Suddenly, surprisingly, there was a line of customers.

' 'Morning, Miss Linette. Your uncle's stuff isn't cheap, is it?'

'It's the best, Mr Chilter—and don't let Uncle Godfrey hear you!' A grunt came wafting over the garden wall and Linette laughed, her eyes lighting up. 'What would you like, Mr Chilter? A cabbage? And some spring onions?' Henry nodded and found some money while she wrapped the goods.

As she handed him the change, a car drew up. It was a blue car, large and, she told herself, as autocratic as its owner. Growing flustered, she dropped the coins among the fruit. Henry laughed, took the two or three she managed to find and waved the rest away.

The young woman was staring at the car, as was the other waiting customer. Linette cleared her throat, attracting the young mother's attention. She jumped and asked for some fruit and vegetables. As she paid, she commented,

'Lovely car, that. Wouldn't mind if my husband owned it.'

Linette stole a glance at the car and hoped the young woman would not notice her flushed cheeks. Two amber eyes were staring straight across the road at her. It seemed she could never do anything to please the man.

'He's the one who wants to get us out,' she informed her customer, then offered the little girl a fruit pastille from a packet. The child filled her mouth and her mother smiled her thanks.

'I heard about that,' the young woman said, starting to walk away. 'Couldn't believe anyone would be so silly as to try to tear your uncle away from his flowers, fruit and vegetables. Not to mention the cottage. We all know how he loves it.'

Linette nodded, then smiled at the third customer of the day. Her hair was not grey, although she was plainly no longer young. Her clothes appeared to be of good quality, her taste quiet. 'I was admiring your display,' the woman said. 'Is this your uncle's handiwork?'

With raised eyebrows and parted lips, Linette nodded.

'How—how did you guess? Oh,' she laughed, 'you heard the people in front of you. Yes, he's very proud of it all. It tastes beautiful,' Linette added, her eyes lifting moment-arily and seeing with relief that the car was moving slowly away.

Her smile touched the woman's serene features, under-standing eyes and surprisingly smooth skin. 'Is it fruit you'd like,' Linette asked, 'or——?'

'I wonder,' the woman ventured quietly, 'if it would be inconveniencing you if I looked around the cottage now?'


## CHAPTER THREE


LINETTE stood like a statue, staring at the woman's face. Now she could see a certain likeness, now she could understand the feeling she had experienced, just for a few seconds, of having seen the woman somewhere.

That 'somewhere', she realised, was in the face and features of her son, Brent Napier. No wonder he was sha-dowing his mother just now in his car—probably making sure, Linette thought, that we didn't set a non-existent dog on her!

It was still difficult to accept the relationship. How much more warmth these eyes held, how much kindliness and sympathy!

'I'm sorry,' the woman was saying, 'if I startled you. To be truthful, I wanted to see you just as you were, you and your uncle.'

Linette came to life, offering her hand over the fruit and lettuces. Then her common sense returned and she came round the stall and held out her hand again. The woman smiled and there was firmness in her grip, a wish to convey friendliness and no hard feelings.

Linette heard herself whisper, as if the woman had actually spoken the words, 'No hard feelings, Mrs Napier.'

The woman smiled with greater certainty. 'Miss Kemp, I'm so happy to meet you. I'd be equally happy to meet your uncle.'

Linette's face grew doubtful and the woman frowned with her. 'Is he really the grumpy man he likes to think he sounds?' Mrs Napier asked.

Linette's laugh was so loud it attracted her uncle's attention. 'You read character well, Mrs Napier. I'll get Uncle Godfrey.' She turned back. 'I'm—I'm sorry about all those comments you must have heard while you were waiting.' She glanced over her shoulder. 'Oh, my uncle's coming.'

Godfrey walked belligerently, head down, cap in his hand. Secretly, Linette wondered at her uncle's unusual courtesy. There were few people indeed to whom he took off his beloved old cap. Nevertheless, it was obvious the meeting was not going to be an easy one.

'Those comments didn't bother me, Miss Kemp,' Mrs Napier was saying. 'In fact, they amused me——'

'Amused you, did they?' Godfrey's gruff voice interrupted. 'They were truly meant, ma'am, and I make no apology for them.'

'Mr Barker?' Mrs Napier's hand came out again, even as she watched Godfrey holding up his own. 'Down-to-earth, honest mud, Mr Barker. It's good stuff. You should see me after a day's gardening!'

Linette had never seen her uncle thrown so off balance. His hand met that of his landlord's mother and Linette judged his grip to be as firm as hers. But it was plain he was not giving in without a fight.

'Flowers you grow, is it?' he queried with a faint derision. 'All pretty and sweet-smelling, for your flower arrangements?'

'I do indeed grow flowers, Mr Barker. But I grow nourishing salads and vegetables, too. Good health comes straight from the ground, that's what I believe.'

'Yes, well . . .' Godfrey glanced, discomfited, at his niece.

'I'll show you round, Mrs Napier.'

'Oh, but your customers——'

Linette shook her head. 'No problem.' She dived under the wooden stall, brought out a notice and propped it in the centre of the display. 'Ring bell for service,' it said. 'If no response, please shout.' Next to it, she placed an old hand-bell.

Mrs Napier smiled and with a friendly nod, followed Linette into the cottage. To Linette's surprise, her uncle joined them, first scraping his boots elaborately on the iron scraper just outside the entrance door. It's the first time, she reflected, I've ever seen him do that.

While Mrs Napier admired the kitchen with its scrubbed look and well-used, though serviceable, modern equipment, Godfrey stood in the doorway. When the visitor's white-sandalled feet trod on the well-worn but still colourful living-room carpet and admired everything she saw, Godfrey watched, hand on armchair, eyes wondering, back stiff with pride.

There was, his niece perceived, a bitter battle taking place inside him. When the visitor admired the polished floorboards, Godfrey looked down at them. As she commented on the tucked-away staircase, he stared at it as if with new eyes.

Linette stood aside to allow Mrs Napier to climb the stairs. At that moment, the hand-bell clanged and a man's voice shouted, 'Service!'

Mrs Napier paused, then looked back at her hostess. 'Please, don't worry about me. Go out to your customer. I can wander about on my own——'

'I'll show the lady round,' Godfrey announced, his voice still gruff. 'I grow my stuff to sell, not to hang around spoiling in the sun.'

'All right, Uncle,' Linette put a placating hand on Godfrey's arm. 'I'm a good saleswoman of your "stuff", aren't I?'

'You're just like your mother,' Godfrey growled. 'Even when she was little, she turned her charms on her big brother—me—and got things out of me.'

'I don't want "things", Uncle. Only a bit of praise.'

Linette's smile widened and her uncle answered, 'You've got that, lass, and you know it.'

Another impatient shout wafted into the cottage. Mrs Napier whispered to Linette, 'The squire of the manor house is demanding your attention, my dear. You'd better do as your uncle says. Knowing my son, he'll stop at nothing to get his own way.' She gave a broad wink which made Linette smile. She went out into the bright sunshine.

The thought came like a cloud-wisp against blue sky. *I wouldn't mind that woman living here.* Looking into the mocking eyes of the woman's son, Linette berated the thought for the treachery it was.

The quizzical smile which greeted her sent her heart into a nose-dive. She was glad her skin was not transparent so that he could see the disruption his mere presence caused to her body's metabolism. She hoped her eyes were not transparent, either, as they clashed with his.

'I only followed instructions,' he commented, gesturing to the notice. 'So why the disapproving look?'

'I was thinking about your mother—about how different she is from you.'

'In a good way, or bad?'

'Much nicer.' Her impudently smiling eyes followed the movement of the fruit she was quite unnecessarily re-arranging. A frown took away the smile. 'Did she approve of your brutal tactics to get my uncle and myself out of the cottage?'

He loomed tall and faintly menacing over the cherished contents of the stall. His mouth had firmed, robbing his face of the trace of indulgence it had held. 'I never answer leading questions, Miss Kemp. I suggest you ask my mother. Whatever I authorised was within the law, and was in fact the only path left to me. Your uncle is an honest man. He's also a stubborn one.'

'Since when has stubbornness made *legalised brutality* an acceptable weapon, Mr Napier?'

His jaw thrust forward and he walked round to her side
of the stall. His thumbs, hooked into his leather belt, drew
attention to the strong width of his hips, the flexing of
muscle in his thighs. His navy shirt was open-necked and
only partially buttoned. Linette's instinct was to back
away, but she forced herself to remain still.

'Don't fight me, Miss Kemp. Right is on my side, not
yours. I also play the tune to which you and, more important, your uncle, have to dance. I could order that heavy-
handed group of men to come back and do their worst,
and no amount of persuasion or abuse on your part would
divert me from my course.'

Linette's gaze was caught and she could not drag it
away.

His hands came to life and gripped her shoulders, pulling
her on a collision-course against his hardness. 'So don't
play with me, either. Don't try my patience, my wide-eyed
friend, nor fling loaded, baiting questions in my face. My
forbearance, in this kind of situation, is fragile indeed.

'I don't want my uncle to lose his home,' she heard her
own voice saying. It was strangely hoarse, little more than
a whisper, and she knew it was the man's nearness, his
latent power reaching out which had almost robbed her of
her voice.

He was not, she vowed, tearing her eyes from his, going
to rob her of her peace of mind, nor upset the equilibrium
of her life.

'What other weapons do I have but verbal ones to defend
our place of living from your grabbing hands?'

Linette rubbed her forehead in a nervous, telling gesture.
He watched the action, hooked his thumbs again and stif-
fened his legs. 'Choose your words more carefully, Miss
Kemp, if you want to keep on the right side of me.'

His glance lingered on her face, moved down the slender,
sun-browned arms to study the clasped hands, empty of
rings. Linette wished her dark blue working overall was
not so all-enveloping, covering the feminine assets she did
possess. She had always dismissed her rounded face and

tip-tilted nose as being so average as to be virtually useless in the mate-acquiring game.

Certainly this man, with his sophisticated tastes—she recalled the careful grooming of his dinner companion—would be less than impressed by her clear skin and blue, laughing eyes, her deeply brown hair cut short and curling waywardly.

His summing-up of her physical qualities remained a mystery since his amber eyes were inscrutable as they lifted. 'You mean,' she challenged, smiling, 'play village maiden to your "local squire" image, Mr Napier?'

'If that's what you want, most certainly. The thought seems to be lodged in your mind, since you're constantly expressing it.'

Linette felt the colour burn her cheeks. Did he think she was after him? 'That's the last thing I'd do,' she declared, putting as much distaste into her expression as she could manage. 'That kiss from you the other day——' How could she tell him, I've been waiting for more ever since?

His eyes hardened. 'You objected to it? We'll make a date some time and I'll improve on it.'

He had it wrong! The distaste in her face must have spilled over into her voice. On second thoughts, she reflected, maybe that was for the best.

'Remember something,' Brent Napier went on. 'Your uncle and aunt were the legal tenants in this cottage. Your aunt, sadly, is no longer here. *You* have no rights in law whatsoever. I could, if I liked, let your uncle stay, but only on condition that he gets rid of you. Bear that in mind the next time you feel the urge to annoy me.'

Her lips pressed together and she started rearranging the vegetables. It was imperative that she kept her hands occupied in order to stop them from making fingernail marks down his arresting but entirely ruthless face.

'You rang for service,' she said sharply. 'If you'll tell me what you want to buy——'

'It's a beautiful cottage,' Mrs Napier was saying as she emerged from the entrance door. As she stood on the path, waiting for Godfrey to join her, she commented, 'It's in a fine state of repair. The flowers, too, the gardens all around it—you've done an excellent job, Mr Barker.'

'So you understand, ma'am, why I'm not going to let any bullies of bailiffs put me and my niece out on the streets?'

'Oh, I do understand, Mr Barker. It would be dreadful if that ever happened.' Mrs Napier spoke abstractedly and looked around, admiration in her gaze.

Linette's astonishment parted her lips and swung her head to Brent Napier. Doesn't your mother know, she wanted to ask, about the terrible way you treated us? She saw her uncle's bewilderment, his foot pushing agitatedly at a clump of grass.

Again Linette looked at Brent. She would *make* him explain, for her uncle's sake. 'What's going to happen about——?'

'My mother has just returned from California,' he stated.

Mrs Napier's head swung back. 'Six months in the sun with my daughter Brenda and her husband, not to mention their three children. Are you a grandfather, Mr Barker?' She was facing Godfrey and smiling.

Linette could see her uncle's embarrassment. She said quickly, 'My aunt wasn't able to have children.'

'I'm so sorry, Mr Barker. I didn't realise . . .' She sought Linette's attention. 'My son wrote often, called me on the telephone even more often.'

Linette gave her full marks for tact. Mrs Napier went on,

'He told me he'd bought a large house in the country, and sold his London house. There were outbuildings at the new place, plus a cottage. I could, if I wanted, indulge my longing for independence and live in the cottage.'

Godfrey grunted, but Mrs Napier did not appear to have heard. Linette, who had expected an outburst, was amazed at her uncle's restraint.

'However,' Mrs Napier concluded brightly, 'it seems

that the cottage already has a very worthy tenant.' She smiled at Godfrey. 'I'm sure my son will allow me to have two or three rooms to myself in the manor house.'

'For the time being, Mother,' was her son's guarded answer, 'that seems to be the only solution.'

Solution, Linette thought, implied a problem—and she was not fooling herself as to what that problem was. Defiant eyes told their landlord that she knew his game and that he hadn't finished with them yet. But now the tactics would have to be different, wouldn't they? With his mother here . . .

'Tomorrow, Mr Barker,' Mrs Napier was saying, 'I'm returning to London. I'll be back, though, and when I come, would you have any objection to my——' Godfrey's expression was alert, like a guard dog on the scent of intruders, 'to my putting on my oldest clothes and helping you in your work? You know, pulling weeds, mowing the lawns? I promise I wouldn't get under your feet.'

Linette laughed, sheer relief lighting her face. Maybe it was intrusion of a kind, but surely her uncle would raise no objection to sacrificing a piece of his garden in exchange for the whole of his cottage?

'You'll do as I say, Mrs Napier,' Godfrey insisted, 'if you bend your back with me over that fine earth!'

'You will give the orders, Mr Barker, I'll carry them out. A gentleman's agreement—purely verbal, nothing written down—but fully honoured nonetheless.'

Godfrey's hand came out. His face bore little expression, but Linette knew his character and could see at a glance how pleased he was.

A sense of victory put mischief into Linette's shining eyes as they turned to the unreadable face of the man who stood beside his mother. We've won, you've lost, her message said clearly. There was no message in return. A blank stare held no comfort, nor did it hold a threat. Yet she was determined to get a reaction of some kind.

'You rang for service, Mr Napier,' she prodded with a smile. 'Can I help you?'

Mrs Napier laughed. 'You have a good saleswoman in your niece, Mr Barker. She's determined to sell the results of your hard work, even if it is to my stony-faced son. Now I wonder,' her eyes, almost as impish as Linette's, scanned his features, 'what's biting him?'

Smiling, lifting her hand to no one in particular, Mrs Napier walked slowly back along the road leading to the house. Godfrey went back to his work, hurrying as if conscious of the time he had spent away from it.

'I should like some flowers,' Brent Napier informed Linette. He indicated the blooms standing in numerous containers. 'Some of each. I don't know their names.'

'Are you particular about colour, Mr Napier? I'm not an experienced florist, but it's important, I think, to match the choice to the recipient. For instance, your mother, and the lady you dined with the other evening——'

'Just make a choice,' Brent interrupted impatiently.

Did his annoyance, she wondered, stem from the length of time the transaction was taking, or her mention of the beautiful woman companion? Anyway, she tried to analyse as she selected the flowers, why had she mentioned her? How this man spent his leisure hours wasn't her concern. A pinpoint of pain, like the prick of a rose thorn, supplied the answer to her question.

'I don't gift-wrap them, Mr Napier,' Linette explained, holding the dripping blooms. 'If you want the trimmings, you'll have to patronise a florist's shop. These are freshly grown by my uncle——'

'Wrap them as you usually do,' he directed, opening his wallet. As she stretched to hand over the flowers, he asked, 'How much?'

Linette named the price, and he gave her the exact amount. She smiled, saying, 'What a pity, no change to throw at you.'

It had been meant as a joke. He took it seriously. 'You'd have done that at your peril.'

He took the path his mother had taken, holding the bunch of blooms with surprising care. They must be intended for his lady friend after all, she surmised, wondering why the day seemed suddenly to have clouded over.

It was after supper that evening that there was a knock on the door. A small boy stood smiling, nursing a bunch of flowers. 'Why, hallo, Jimmy,' Linette said. 'What have you got there?'

'Flowers, Miss Lin. For you. From the big house up there.' He moved his elbow in the direction of the side road.

'Thanks a lot for bringing them, Jimmy.' Linette had recognised them as those she had that morning sold to Brent Napier. The boy ran off and Linette closed the door.

There was a swinging note attached which ran, 'For Linette Kemp, who should remember that she, as a sub-tenant, has no security of tenure whatsoever. B.N.'

The card she tore with furious movements into small pieces, pushing them into a pocket.

She would not tell her uncle about the card. The flowers, which he would recognise, she would say had appeared to have come from an unknown admirer, since there had been no name attached—which she argued, was partially true. He would ask her who had patronised the stall that day and she would tell him there had been so many customers, she could not clearly remember.

'Unknown admirer', she reflected, opening the living-room door, was an irony. Not only did the sender not admire her, it would seem he disliked her so much, he had every intention of putting her out on to the streets.

It was impossible to escape the fact that she was at the mercy of a man who had no mercy, and that was the greatest irony of all.

The play-group started again. Linette telephoned the mothers and assured them that there would be no repeat of the disastrous circumstances which had caused them to withdraw their children. They were relieved to hear the

news and seemed delighted to be able to bring their offspring again.

Leslie was pleased, too. 'Which morning shall I bring
Jenny?' he asked.

'Tomorrow. The sooner we resume the better for everyone. We've met Mr Napier's mother,' she confided, as her
uncle sat reading the paper. 'She's so nice, Leslie, I
couldn't believe it!'

'When's she moving in?' Leslie asked.

'No mention of that. We couldn't understand it. She
said she's going to share her son's house. According to her
wonderful son,' Linette had intended to infuse sarcasm
into the descriptive word, but for some reason, it just
wouldn't come, 'it's just a temporary arrangement.'

As she rang off, she thought, Do I really believe that
impossible man is 'wonderful'? It was true that even though
he was away, having gone with his mother to London, she
could not get the man out of her mind.

She felt no safer in her uncle's cottage for the landlord's
absence. The man was capable of issuing orders to her
through his lawyers, dislodging her from her home without
feeling or pity.

It was a joyful moment when the children came running
along the path to the cottage door. Linette's arms were
opened wide and each of the six children ran for a quick
hug. Their mothers went away with a wave. Leslie, Jenny's
father, lingered.

'Would you come round this evening, Linette? Just an
hour or two, for a chat.' Her hesitation was slight, but he
noticed. 'I get lonely. And I've missed you. I haven't liked
to come here while there was that trouble.'

Mine isn't over yet, she thought, but could not tell him.
Not even her uncle knew of Brent Napier's threats.

The appeal in Leslie's eyes had her nodding. 'Uncle
Godfrey will probably go out for an evening drink to meet his
friends. I'll be round as soon as I've tidied up after our meal.'

Leslie squeezed Linette's arm. There was a spring in his
step as he returned to his car.

Linette went out before her uncle did, after all. There was a comedy programme on television which he wanted to watch, he told her. Only half an hour, then he'd pop round to the pub.

It was a warm evening. The sun was lowering from a pearl-blue sky, bronzing everything it touched. It enhanced the golden-grey walls of the old houses, changed subtly the shades of the flowers which grew profusely in front gardens and spilled over the small, rectangular flower-beds jutting from houses to stone pavements.

Leslie's little house was one of a terrace along the main road. Outside the bay window was a wooden box filled with scarlet flowers. It was Jenny's job, Linette had been informed by the proud little girl, to take care of the flowers. 'Until my mummy comes home,' she had said with pride and a touch of wistfulness.

Jenny was in bed but awake when Linette arrived. A high-pitched voice summoned her upstairs and Linette received back the hug she had given the child that morning. When Linette turned to go, Jenny cried out, 'Stay with me, Linette. Tell me a story. I'm not sleepy . . .'

Hating to disappoint any child, Linette took a deep breath, was about to agree but started to listen to her own reason. Stay out of Leslie's problems, it warned. Don't take the place of her mother as she's trying to make you do.

Leslie's eyes revealed his secret hopes, also. It wouldn't do, it simply would not do! Shaking her head, she returned to the bed and hugged Jenny tightly. 'Cuddle your teddy bear or your panda and you tell *them* a story, Jenny. Remember the one I told you this morning?' Jenny nodded, disappointment in her drooping mouth. 'Tell them that story, darling.'

Linette backed away, preceding Leslie out of the room and calling 'goodnight'.

Half-way through the evening Leslie suggested that they went out for a drink. 'I'll ask the neighbour to come in for an hour. She's willing to baby-sit at any time.'

Since the conversation between them was threatening to
dry up, having exhausted every topic on which, in the
circumstances, it was permissible to speak, Linette agreed.
Eagerly, Leslie called on his neighbour, while Linette
gazed at a family photograph. Leslie's wife was young and
sweet, Leslie himself the picture of happiness. Jenny stood,
laughing, between them.

Leslie returned, holding out his hand. Linette did not
take it. She went out to the street, waiting while he locked
the door. 'I've given the neighbour a key,' he said.

It was the George and Dragon they went to, which was
the local inn to which her uncle had referred. Leslie showed
Linette to a table, circular and polished so that its dark,
uneven wood shone. It was scattered with beer mats and
Linette played nervously with hers while she waited for
Leslie as he ordered drinks at the bar.

It was impossible to explain to herself why she was nervous. Had the incident of the local men going to her uncle's
cottage with the intention of putting him out caused her to
distrust even those she regarded as friends?

There was a burst of laughter and she twisted in her
seat. Her uncle was there and he had seen her. She
answered his salute of recognition with a wave of her own.
Those around him waved, too. It seemed he had forgotten
and forgiven those men, for he was surrounded by them.

Leslie returned with the drinks, lowering them carefully
to the table. For a while, they drank in silence. It seemed
to Linette that there was something on Leslie's mind.

He took a swallow of beer, found the beer mat with the
base of the glass and said, 'Jane's asked me for a divorce—
when the two years are up, that is.'

'How long now, Leslie?' Linette asked sympathetically.

'Five months.'

'So there's a long way to go before you can do anything
about it.'

Leslie nodded. 'I don't want a divorce, Lin.'

'You mean you still love her?'

His face lifted at last, but it held despair. 'How can I,

the way she treated me? I'm thinking of Jenny. Lin——.'
he grew red, his fingers gripped the glass, 'you wouldn't
think of coming to live——'

'Live with you?' She had not intended the dismay to
show. 'But Leslie, I couldn't do that. I don't l——'

'Love me. Okay, I accept that, and I didn't mean it
that way. Just—just live in my house, be a mother to
Jenny.' Linette knew that Leslie had realised just what he
was asking of her. His hand covered hers as it rested on her
lap. 'Sorry, Lin. Forget it.'

Linette nodded quickly, wishing he would remove his
hand. It stayed there and she looked anxiously across the
crowded place at her uncle, hoping he was too absorbed in
his friends' conversation to notice. With relief, she saw that
he was laughing at someone's joke. He had not seen—but
someone else had.

On a stool at the bar, in a darkened corner, Brent
Napier sat alone, a glass of beer to his lips, his coolly
appraising eyes gazing at her over the rim.

So their landlord and tormentor was back from London.
His reappearance, Linette was sure, heralded a shattering
of their peace—and her own peace of mind. His expression
was as hard, at that moment, as the day he had stood and
watched as the bailiffs had started to ransack the cottage.

I haven't forgiven him for that act of calculated cruelty,
she told herself fiercely. So why should I care how he
regards me because I allow my friend's hand to hold mine?
All the same, she eased her hand from Leslie's, annoyed
with herself even as she did so.

'What's wrong, Lin?' Leslie asked, then remarked with
surprise, 'Your uncle's getting a refill. He's talking to Mr
Napier. I thought he was on bad terms with him—you,
too.'

'I certainly am,' Linette answered. 'I can't speak for my
uncle. Mr Napier's mother seems to have made him go soft
towards the Napier family.'

'Mrs Napier's going to take over the cottage after all?
And your uncle's going to leave just like that—even after

the stand he took against the bailiffs?'

'No, no! I'm the one Mr Napier's after, now. He says I'm a sub-tenant——'

'Which you are,' Leslie put in logically.

'I know. He also says that as such, I have no legal rights and that he can get me out at any time.' She added bitterly, 'As if I didn't know. Every time I see the man, I can—I can almost feel him grab my hair and pull me out of the cottage with it.'

'Cave man stuff?' Leslie commented with a smile.

Linette nodded, hoping to hide the shiver—surely it wasn't of anticipation?—running through her body. 'More feudal lord, really.' Her smile was strained. 'You know, "having his will of the young, innocent peasant girl".'

Leslie laughed. Even over the raised voices of the drinkers, the sound of his laughter drew brief, interested glances. Linette shot a quick look at the two men talking at the bar. Brent Napier was standing now, his elbow on the high counter, his hip pressed negligently against it.

His head was returning as if in the wake of a measured look in their direction. Her uncle was bent forward, his elbows supporting him. There was a full glass in front of him, a half-filled glass in Brent Napier's hand.

Linette wished she could see her uncle's face. His companion's seemed serious enough. Although they did not look at her, she felt that their discussion somehow concerned her future. When her uncle shook his head, she sensed he was not conveying a negative message, but one of uncertainty, even doubt.

'You don't think he'll exercise his legal rights, though, do you, Lin?' Leslie interrupted her thoughts.

'In making me leave, but allowing Uncle Godfrey to stay?' Linette shrugged, turning her empty glass in stiff fingers. 'What good would that do him? He said he wanted the cottage empty. My leaving——'

'Would mean one less person to deal with.'

'Maybe.' She sighed, wishing she could see into the future—her own.

'You'll need to do a lot of talking.' Godfrey's voice drifted over. Brent Napier's lips moved. Linette wished she could lip-read, but her uncle's plain-speaking saved her the bother.

'Persuasion?' Godfrey remarked. He shook his head again and this time it took the form of an unequivocal 'no'. 'My niece is too like me. With her, it's honesty and openness all the way.' He made to move back to his seat. 'I'll have to do a lot of thinking, Mr Napier, a lot of thinking.'

Godfrey turned in Linette's direction as he eased his way between the tables. He made a brief toasting gesture with his glass and moved on.

'Now I wonder what that was all about,' Linette mused.

'Looks like you'll know in a minute,' Leslie commented. 'He's coming over. Want me to go, Linette?'

'No, no, please stay, Leslie.' She panicked at the thought of being left alone with Brent Napier. He was, she was certain, about to wreak havoc on her uncle's and her own settled way of life. Not only that, she thought, with a touch of fear, with my nervous system, too. Why else was her heart starting to pound, her teeth gnawing at her lower lip?

'Refill, Miss Kemp? Mr Dickens?' Brent's question was short and to the point.

'I'll get them.' Leslie pushed back his chair. 'You, too, Mr Napier?' Brent held up his glass which was half full.

Linette looked up, surprised by Leslie's unaccustomed act of taking the initiative in such a situation. His expression told her his reason—the desire to escape from Brent Napier's presence. Linette couldn't blame him, since she was experiencing the same feeling herself.

Attack, she decided, was the only weapon she possessed against this formidable man. 'Have you been trying to talk my uncle into telling me to go back home, Mr Napier?' His raised eyebrows indicated his displeasure at her bluntness. The reaction incited her to continue. 'After all, you did say the other day you could make it a condition of his staying on that he got rid of me.'

With his foot, Brent jerked round a wooden chair and occupied it, lowering his glass to the table. 'I know I did. I also warned you not to play with me, or to try my patience by asking loaded questions.'

Linette looked anxiously for Leslie. He was leaning on the bar counter, awaiting his turn to be served. He was prepared, it seemed, to wait until closing time, if necessary.

Brent Napier followed her eyes. 'Is your boy-friend's wife baby-sitting while he spends the evening with you?'

Linette turned on him. 'Now who's asking the loaded questions? Leslie's wife has left him. If I befriend a lonely man——'

A sarcastic eyebrow lifted. 'Is that what it's called in your world? In the big world outside, it has another name.' With his eyes still on her, he tossed the remaining contents of his glass down his throat.

He lowered the glass with a thump to the table, then let his eyes linger on her profile. 'You haven't thanked me for the flowers I sent you.'

Linette caught the glimmer of amusement. 'I loved the flowers,' she answered promptly, 'but I hated the note the sender attached to them.'

'Did you hate the sender, too?'

If only my heart wasn't pounding, Linette panicked. If only my thoughts weren't entwining themselves around his hard body, snaking round his neck and entangling with his dark hair. If she'd had them under control, she reasoned, she could without a twinge of conscience, tell him 'Yes'.

Instead, she responded tartly, 'Surely you know the answer to that, Mr Napier, without my having to put it into words?'

'Lin?' Leslie placed her drink in front of her. 'Sorry I was so long. This place is busy tonight.'

Brent's eyebrows moved upwards again in derisive comment as he scanned the empty bar counter. 'You're right, Mr Dickens. It's a wonder you survived the crush.' He stood, easing back his chair. He nodded to Leslie, threw a twisted smile at Linette and wished them goodnight.

# CHAPTER FOUR

GODFREY called from the door, 'Just going out for a drink, Linette. If you need me, you know where to find me.'

From the room used by the play-group, Linette called out in reply. For a few moments she stopped dusting and stared through the low-silled window. Outside, her uncle's vegetable plot flourished. Beyond that, and beyond the low wall defining the boundary of the garden, stretched part of the wooded and cultivated parkland belonging to the big house which belonged to the Napiers.

Its name was Wealden Grange and Linette supposed it was once the manor house. She tried to imagine the people who had inhabited it when it was built in the early years of the seventeeth century. Had the squire been as imperious as the present owner? Was he successful in his dealings with merchants, making his money that way? Or had he inherited his fortune?

To own and maintain such a place, she mused, he would have needed a great deal of money, even in those days. There was no doubting the financial status of the man whose house it was now. He had inherited a fortune in the shape of a successful company—or rather, group of companies.

Her eyes dropped back to the thriving garden, and she thought about her uncle's unusually withdrawn behaviour in the last day or so—ever since he had chatted to Brent Napier over a drink. A number of times he had appeared to be starting to speak to her, but a curious reticence had overcome his habitual openness.

'Why the sigh?' The mocking question came from the doorway. Linette swung round, knowing at once who it was, yet looking at him as if he were a stranger. Dressed casually, the real strength of the man came through as it never had in formal attire.

'Do you have a secret longing to have the right to call those grounds and woodlands your own? Not to mention the house?'

With the back of her wrist, she shifted some stray curls from her face. 'The comfort and peace of a country cottage is all I ask of life, Mr Napier. It's what I have, sharing it with my uncle, and it's what I intend to keep.'

Her blue eyes challenged—until he moved. He came only a pace or two nearer, yet the fluidity of his movement, the latent power in the breadth of his shoulders, revealed by the stretch of the dark green shirt, caused her bold gaze to falter and turn to one of fear.

It was his ability to make her bones turn to water that frightened her. Or had they turned to wine? Something seemed to have gone to her head, because all she could think of was how it had felt to be pulled against him that day he had ordered the bailiffs into the cottage.

'I shouldn't bank on it, Miss Kemp,' he said softly. Did he know how he made her feel? He held her defensive gaze hard and long. When he had seemingly grown tired of the silent by-play, he looked away, round the room, into the opened cupboards.

He looked up, finding her eyes still on him. Linette coloured and turned away, hoping to hide it. If only I didn't find him so—so magnetic, she thought desperately. How can you fight a man who haunts you when he's not here, yet torments you with his elusiveness when he is?

'Those toys—they're a bit battered, aren't they?' Was he deliberately baiting her?

'They've been well used. I've bought them at local garden fêtes, or made them myself. I put out a box of sand when the children come, and when it's fine, I give them a tin bath of water outside.'

'Haven't you got any other equipment, something the kids can let off steam with?'

'Slides, climbing frames and so on?' He nodded and she faced him, putting aside the duster. 'Of course not. They cost money, and I just don't have enough of it to buy such things. But you wouldn't understand that, would you, Mr Napier?'

His eyes narrowed but he made no attempt to put her down for what he clearly regarded as an impudent remark. 'You must have saved a reasonable amount from the money you charge the children's mothers.'

'I don't charge. It's a play-group, not a play school. And I'm not a qualified teacher or a nursery nurse. I take the children in for two hours three mornings a week to give their mothers a respite, or a chance to go shopping on their own.'

'I suppose your uncle pays you nothing, either?'

'For helping him? It's not really your business, Mr Napier,' she spoke calmly, 'but you're right. I pay him instead—rent and money for my keep.'

'A real live philanthropist in front of me. Right on my doorstep, too. I suppose it's all just a labour of love to you.'

'Yes, it is.' Her flushed face rose to his. 'I enjoy helping my uncle. I like selling his produce and working hard with him to grow it. And it's one of my greatest pleasures to have the children here, keeping them happy, teaching them the fundamentals of a good life—such as working together in harmony.'

'Your ideals are to be admired, Miss Kemp.' She knew he intended no praise when his mouth curved into the shadow of a smile. 'You'll make a good mother one day. When your boy-friend's wife divorces him and you marry him, you'll have a ready-made family on your hands, won't you.'

Linette frowned, then felt the anger rising, 'For the record, Mr Napier, he's a *friend*, no more, no less.'

'But of course.'

She could have thrown the duster at him for his disbelief. He strolled to the window, the hands in his slacks pockets drawing attention to the leanness of his hips. For a moment, Linette allowed herself to study the breadth of his shoulders, the confident, straight-backed posture, then resumed her dusting.

'Will you spare an evening away from your *friend* and have a meal with me tomorrow night?'

The invitation had her scrabbling on the carpet for a child's apron she had been folding. 'Why——?' She stopped, her face flushed both from bending and confusion. He swung from the window, his expression daring her to refuse. 'Why not?' she ventured, swiftly changing her approach.

A passing amusement softened his mouth, but he only nodded in response to her over-bright acceptance. Her eyes were still bright when he called for her next evening. It was Saturday, but her uncle had, to her surprise, delayed going to meet his friends for the customary chat.

When she saw him watching Brent's arrival with a look which said nothing, yet spoke volumes, she experienced the deepest suspicion that the invitation had been part of the 'persuasion' of which her uncle had spoken.

With a nod, Godfrey left them, passing them in the entrance hall on his way to the door. Brent looked her over and Linette wondered if the simplicity of her pink-patterned, ankle-length dress, with its short sleeves and vee-neck, would provoke a slightly contemptuous reaction.

'Do I match up to your lady companion of the other evening, Mr Napier? Or would you like me to dash upstairs and change my dress for a more sophisticated one, and while I'm there, change my personality to match?'

His smile did not convey amusement. 'Are you out to rile me?'

'No, only to try and tell you in advance that I'm not open to persuasion *of any sort*.'

An eyebrow lifted. 'Persuasion? What kind did you have in mind? An end-of-evening love scene? Or, as you would put it, the obnoxious squire and helpless young peasant routine?'

Linette could not suppress a smile. 'I doubt if my uncle would condone that, and he was the one who used the word "persuasion" the other night, while he was speaking to you.'

His answer was a vague, 'Ah, now I get it,' and a glance at his watch, followed by a polite, 'Shall we go?' He stood back to allow her to pass through the door.

Linette paused, searching in vain for Brent's car. She looked at him questioningly.

'We'll walk,' he said, turning left and inviting her to follow. They passed by the side of the flower garden adjoining her uncle's cottage and made their way along the lane marked 'Private Road' which led to Wealden Grange.

Tall trees met overhead, forming a kind of extended archway. Leaves rustled, and the air was full of country evening scents. Brent's hands were in his pockets and his eyes were strangely preoccupied with the road surface. His mind, Linette sensed, was far away, but it appeared she was wrong, since he looked at her with a fleeting smile as if he had guessed she had been watching him.

'In answer to your question,' he commented, 'no, you don't even begin to compare with Nita Cutler, the woman I dined with.'

An unreasoning disappointment gave rise in her mind to an irrational sense of inadequacy. Immediately on the defensive, she opened her mouth to attack when she stumbled over a stone. Brent's hand shot out to steady her and she stopped. The muscles in her akle had been over-stretched as her foot had turned and she stooped to rub it.

'Something wrong?' He crouched and to steady herself, she held his shoulder. He pushed away her massaging fingers and held her ankle firmly.

'It's not sprained,' she said, agitated by the gentleness of his hands. 'It's better now, honestly it is.'

His eyes lifting to hers were flecked with the gold-on-blue glow of the setting sun. There was mocking amusement in the mixture, too. 'I didn't realise,' he remarked, 'that my touch held such curative powers.'

He released her ankle and straightened. At once, Linette missed the probing, rubbing warmth of his hands. 'Now, where were we?' he queried with a smile and walked on more slowly. 'I was saying you didn't resemble in the slightest——' his arm went round her waist as if to prevent yet another stumble, 'the woman I——'

'If my appearance is so unsatisfactory,' Linette snapped defensively, 'I'll relieve you of my company.' She stood still. 'Here and now.'

He walked on a pace or two, turned and faced her. His curved forefinger lifted her chin. 'You look charming, and this evening I want your company more than anyone else's in the world. Now, will you stay with me?'

Linette nodded, knowing the statement wasn't really true. She kept strictly to herself the fact that she wanted *his* company more than any other man's. How, she asked her irritated second self, am I expected to resist that special look in those curiously translucent brown eyes? The irresistible smile which he can turn on like a switch flicking?

Remember the other, rock-hard man inside the charming façade, her interior argument persisted. Remember the ruthless creature who, if it hadn't been for her pleas, would have had her uncle thrown out, along with his possessions, from the cottage he had cherished for so many years.

Linette was on her guard, then, as the memory of her uncle's horror and helplessness returned. 'I'll stay with you,' she agreed, 'but only to humour you. If I refuse, you might return to your "wicked landlord" skin and threaten——'

'You're so right,' he drawled. He had stopped again and was looking her over. His smile was slow, his expression wicked. 'You've given me a weapon, Miss Kemp, a threat to hold over you continually. My demands——'

Linette swung round and started to run. He caught her easily, gripping her wrist and turning her back to walk beside him. His fingers slid down, found hers and pushed

through them, holding them fast. They were linked,
judging by the strength of his hold, for all time.

'Try to escape now,' he baited.

Taking him at his word, Linette attempted to disengage.
'It's like being handcuffed to you,' she complained.

'Good. Consider yourself tied to me for——' he considered her again, eyes narrow, 'for as long as I fancy you.'

Her tug to free herself only inflicted pain—on her own
fingers and arm. 'A—a man like you couldn't fancy a
girl like me. After seeing you with the woman you called
Nita——'

'Ah, Nita Cutler. Now she is something——'

'Out of this world,' Linette took him up acidly.

'Knows a man's needs, anticipates them . . .' Another
tug was easily stilled by him. 'Business woman to the core.'

'She works——?' There was a note of near-horror in
Linette's voice.

'In my company. Top secretary, handles clients——'

'And boss,' Linette interpolated.

'And boss,' his look was faraway, 'superbly.'

'You mean,' Linette queried hoarsely, 'she's your
secretary?'

'Not mine.' He smiled, yet managed to sound sad at
the same time. 'One of the company's top executives.'

'But she was dining with *you*.'

'Why not? I'm not tied in any way. Why should I not
take out a beautiful woman?'

'Especially one who *anticipates a man's needs*.' Linette's
sour tone hung on the evening sweetness, corroding it.
There was no answer from her companion, so she added,
'I'm the complete opposite of her, so what am I doing here
with you, wasting your evening?'

'I like to put my dates in a box, shake them about to
mix them and take out the first name that comes.'

Before she could find a suitable retort, they were walking, still hand in hand, through a doorway in the high
stone wall which denoted one part of the estate's limit.
Beside the door were locked, seemingly impenetrable gates.

These, she assumed, were opened only when the owner and the owner's guests came and went.

As Brent turned to secure the door behind them, Linette gazed with a rush of aesthetic pleasure at the honey-coloured Cotswold stone of which the manor house was built. Its gold-tone was highlighted by the reflected paint-box colours of the setting sun. The panes of glass in the stone mullioned windows also took into themselves the evening's brightness.

'It's all so lovely,' she murmured, her gaze shifting to sweep over parkland, lawns and ancient trees.

'It is.'

Something in his tone made her look at him, only to find his eyes were on her. She coloured and hoped he would think her face was, like the many windows, reflecting back the sky's brilliance. How could she keep to herself the way he affected her, even a look from him having the power to break through her antagonism?

'Where are we eating?' she asked lightly, feeling the need to say something to break the difficult silence. 'At your house?'

'Would you have preferred me to have booked a table somewhere?'

The slow shake of her head disguised her pulse's leap of pleasure at the thought of dining alone with him in the intimate atmosphere of his home.

It seemed, however, that his home was not the place he had in mind. He gestured to the left, to a wide and winding path which was once, no doubt, used by horse-drawn wagons, by barking dogs on their way to help in the fields, and by heavily-shod farm labourers tramping over it on their walk to tend the animals in the estate's distant pastures.

Now it seemed to lead to a broken circle of trees. Puzzled, Linette walked at Brent Napier's side, taking care not to stumble on the hard, rutted track. She did not want his hand shooting out again to keep her from falling. She didn't want to do anything which would make him look at her with mocking suspicion, as if she had manipulated a near-fall so as to attract his attention.

When the cottage came into view, she gasped, 'That's the one you photographed and showed us the before-and-after pictures!' They had stopped and something in her reached out to the place, the warmth of welcome that it radiated even to a stranger. as she was.

Its construction was of the warm Cotswold stone, but it did not have the stone-tiled roof of her uncle's cottage. Instead, it was newly thatched, so neatly and so attractively that it could only have been the work of a thatching expert of modern times. It did not have the pointed gables over the dormer windows of the other cottage. Its windows were, instead, inset and protected by the jutting thatching.

'Are we dining there?' Linette asked eagerly.

'I'm glad you're pleased,' was the dry reply. 'I thought you might in your usual rebellious way take offence and fling your "feudal" speech in my face.' He waited for her reaction, but she merely smiled. 'I should have explained that my house is undergoing extensive renovation. I have two or three rooms for my own use. My mother, when she's here, has a couple more at her disposal.'

'I don't mind,' Linette assured him, 'I don't mind at all.' Her nod indicated the building among the trees. 'I love it. It's been so well restored it's kept its history, yet it invites twentieth-century man—and woman—to come right in.'

'Please do just that, twentieth-century woman.' He smiled broadly and Linette felt her heart trip and recover, only to beat the faster for its falter at the charm he had, without warning, turned on her. Could this smiling man really be the one who had stood relentlessly watching as the bailiffs, under his instructions, had tramped into their home?

They walked straight into the living-room. The floor-boards had been stained and polished and scattered with expensive rugs. The furniture, with its patterned covers, the matching lined curtains, blended perfectly with the time-mellowed atmosphere created by the wooden beams and wide, welcoming hearth.

At the end of the through-room, near to doors plainly fitted in modern times, stood a table set for two. Red candles poised unlighted in their holders, scarlet napkins expertly rolled, stood on side plates. The central light was out, leaving wall lights to illuminate the room.

'Who——?' Linette began, but her question was unnecessary. A round-faced young woman put her head round the partly-opened door.

'Shall I bring it in, Mr Napier?' At his nod, she said, ' 'Evening, Miss Kemp.'

'Mary!' Linette exclaimed. 'I didn't expect to see you here.'

'I clean and cook for Mr Napier, Miss Kemp. And his mother, when she's here. I'll get the food.' She withdrew and her feet bustled away.

'While we're waiting,' Brent Napier said, 'would you like a drink?' As Linette shook her head, he invited, 'Come and see the other room.'

'It's a larger cottage than I thought,' Linette commented, following him through a doorway and appreciating as she went the inviting aroma from the kitchen. 'Oh, isn't this pleasant?' The room she gazed around was furnished as comfortably, if a little more sparsely, as the other.

'The furnishings and so on are my mother's taste. The brick surround of the fireplace was her suggestion, too.'

Linette nodded, then frowned. 'If your mother has taken such an interest in this place, Mr Napier, why doesn't she live here instead of——'

'My name's Brent.' He smiled faintly. 'Please call me that.'

'Mr Napier,' she repeated stubbornly.

His shoulders lifted. 'If you insist. But don't blame me, will you, for adhering to the "squire and tenant" roles.' His smile this time was one of 'Check. Your move.' He was right. He had put her in a corner.

A sharp sigh preceded her capitulation. 'Brent.'

'Linette,' he countered, softly.

This time her breath was indrawn, slowly, as she tried with lightning speed to sort through the jumble of feelings his first-time use of her name had aroused. It was impossible to deny that she wanted to hear him speak it again—and again.

'You haven't answered my question,' she responded, changing the subject in her own mind. 'Why doesn't your mother come and live here?'

'Mr Napier,' Mary's voice sang from the near-distance. As they emerged into the hall, she added, 'Don't let the food get cold.'

As Linette took her place at the table, and watched Mary put a match to the candles, she knew she could not ask her question for the third time.

The conversation over the excellent soup was stiff and difficult. It was not until the wine Brent had poured to accompany the first course began to sing through Linette's body that her mind relaxed.

'That's better,' said her host after a while. 'I'm conversing with a warm human being now instead of a stone replica of the female of the species.'

Linette smiled and relaxed even further. 'Sorry, Mr——' She checked, and continued, 'Brent.' Her eyes sought his over the rim of the hastily seized wine glass. To her surprise, she saw he was smiling broadly.

'Well done,' was his softly sarcastic rejoinder.

'The—the food is excellent.' It was the first thing she could think of with which to change the conversation's direction.

'Finished?' Mary asked from the door. 'My, Miss Kemp, you must have been hungry. Every bit's gone.'

'My guest has told me, Mary, that she thinks the meal is excellent.'

Mary blushed. 'Oh, good,' she said, then added a little ruefully, 'It should be. I've had enough practice, me with four kids.' She grinned. 'Coffee over there, Mr Napier?'

Slightly to Linette's consternation, Brent joined her on the couch. He lounged back, legs stretched, shoulders against the upholstery. He watched as Linette poured.

Handing Brent a cup, Linette took a sip from her own. Without looking at him, she remarked, 'I'm enjoying your methods of persuasion—Brent.' How strange it was to speak his name. 'But I'm not sure where it's all leading?'

It had been intended as a faintly amused comment, but it had emerged as an apprehensive question. Her cup met the saucer with a rattle, giving away her growing agitation at his proximity. The jacket of his suit had fallen open, and she had an almost improper urge to throw herself on to him and hug his waist, letting her head press against the wide expanse of his chest.

When he lowered his clasped hands from behind his head, she jumped, thinking he had interpreted her thoughts and was prepared to receive her self-sacrificial action with alacrity. Only it wouldn't have involved any sacrifice on her part, she thought. It would have been a pleasure, a delight . . .

'Something wrong?' The familiar words came softly, insinuatingly.

He had used those words before, earlier, when her foot had turned while walking along the road towards his house. Then, he had bent to massage her ankle, but he certainly couldn't massage her mind, attempting to take away the pain of sudden knowledge—that her feelings had played traitor and led her along the perilous path of starting to care deeply for a man who wished her nothing but harm.

'Excuse me interrupting,' Mary spoke from the door, 'but can I clear away? Finished your coffee?'

Brent nodded and thanked her, waiting for the clatter of dishes to end. As Mary retreated backwards into the kitchen, he told her to leave the dishes. Mary thanked him, saying, 'I'll wash them in the morning.' A few minutes later she called 'goodnight' and tapped her way down the path.

Linette stood up, straightening her skirt. 'I must go. My uncle will——'

His hand tugged her back beside him. 'Your uncle won't. Be still, fidget. My dinner guests don't up and leave with the domestic help.'

The thought of the next hour or two alone with him was so unnerving, she burst out, 'There's nothing else to do. We've eaten, I've dined with you——' There was a brief silence and she heard again her own words. 'I'm sorry to sound so ungracious.'

'You were, but I'll forgive you—this time.' His hand ran lightly down her bare arm, making her shiver, but she held herself stiffly. 'As I forgave you the times when you've so rudely called me names.'

'You deserved them.'

A hand flicked a curl, but she jerked away. Brent lifted himself to his feet and wandered across the room. Linette watched him go, her heart in her eyes, having, she was sure, leapt itself there from its rightful place inside her. He was peeling off his jacket and loosening his tie.

If she ran out . . . He would laugh, probably call her a frightened virgin. She sank back. It wouldn't, she reflected, be far from the truth. She *was* frightened of him, of the power he wielded over her reflexes.

It wasn't fair, she mused. He was determined to eliminate her uncle and herself from his life and wished them no good at all. So why, she fretted, did he have to be so attractive, so tall, his build so strong, his features so pleasant to look at?

Resting back, she simulated the attitude of a perfectly relaxed woman, but when the strains of music, classical, persuasively melodious, drifted into the room, her body stiffened, letting her down.

He was seated beside her now and once more his arm pressed hers. He stretched out his legs and there was no falseness about his relaxed pose. A hand crept across the back of her neck, bringing tingles to her skin. The hand lowered to the small of her back, lingered there—was he giving her time to protest?—then pushed its way across until his arm was round her waist.

Her lips compressed as her breathing became tight. She was fighting him—and fighting the music, too.

'Linette?' His head turned against the back of the couch. His eyelids drooped lazily, resting on her face.

A flame flickered inside her, smaller, more darting than those of the candles which had burned on the table. 'Brent?' she answered in a whisper.

His hand pulled her closer, cupping her breast. Still he regarded her, waiting, waiting . . . There was nothing she could do but stiffen and say, with a strangely parched mouth, 'No, Brent, no!'

His hand did not move. Her heart beat strengthened, causing her blood to race around her veins. A trail of fire, started by that first tiny flame, was scorching through her. With all her strength she fastened on that wayward hand of his, pulling at it in jerks, but it would not move. Instead, its hold grew stronger—and more audacious, finding its way round the barrier of her dress.

Refusing to admit defeat, she paused, steeled herself against the insinuating magic his slowly moulding fingers against her soft flesh were causing and made a thrust with words. 'Is this part of your *persuasion* plan?' The point of her cutting remark must have been blunted, since it bounced off him.

Panic started hammering at the pulse in her throat. The sound of the music was soaking into her brain, combining with his lips which were skimming over her neck and his hand, knowledgeably gentling her, to bring about a melting of her limbs and a lethargy which was threatening to close her mind down for the night.

If she didn't break free now . . . I don't want to break free, she thought, and moments later, was past the point of exercising her reason. When he moved her nearer, she went willingly. When his hands turned her towards him, then slid round her to encase her in bands of iron, she had no resistance left to offer.

His kiss when it came was light and teasing and so unlike the first time it took her by surprise. She found herself wanting more, parting her lips expectantly in involuntary invitation. He needed no further encouragement. His mouth descended and took over hers, tasting the untried moistness and plainly liking its heady flavour.

His hands moved over her, momentarily covering her breasts, then moving to grip her under the arms. Pressed against the hardness of him, she could inhale the faint aroma which came from the freshness of his skin, as if showers and soap and cleanliness were part of his daily life.

By now her arms were crossed behind his neck. Her eyes were closed and her mouth the bruised and hungry recipient of his kisses. Never stop, she thought, never stop kissing me. Perversely, at that moment he lifted his head.

Their eyes met and she saw that he had caught her fire. His were burning gold and desire blazed from them. Hers, to him, must have seemed dazed, since that, she told herself, was exactly how she was feeling.

'How—how did this happen?' she asked falteringly, then moved an arm from around him to finger her mouth. 'My lips are sore,' she said wonderingly. 'You did that to them.'

'And didn't you love it, sweetheart?'

Still lying against him, she frowned. Even in her drunken-like stupor, the word 'sweetheart' seemed misplaced. 'I'm not your sweetheart,' she protested. 'All you've done is kiss me——'

Sparkling eyes topped his slow smile. 'You're wanting more?' He made as if to push her off his lap. 'You're welcome, Miss Kemp, you're very welcome. The bedroom is up those wooden stairs over there.'

'That's not what I meant,' she retorted, 'and I'm sure you know it.'

He laughed, his head back, and she felt the urge to reach up and touch his throat, trace his thrusting chin and jawline. Her hand clenched to keep it from taking such a liberty.

'Come with me,' he pushed her gently and she scrambled to her feet. 'I'll show you the bedroom.'

Linette attempted to free herself from his hold on her arm. 'No, thank you. Did I forget to inform you that I'm not that kind of female?'

'So imperious she is in defence of her virtue!' .

He was laughing at her and she looked around for her bag. He saw the action. 'No, you don't,' he stated firmly. His hand found hers and entwined with it. They were fused together again as they had been earlier. 'You have my solemn promise that all we'll do is look at it.'

Believing him implicitly, she allowed him to lead her to the stairs. When their hands parted in order to climb to the next floor, Linette felt a sense of disappointment.

The bedroom was all a cottage bedroom should be, she thought, gazing round. It was not large, but it was a tasteful mixture of past and present. The wooden floorboards with scattered rugs, were stained dark brown and shone in the remaining light from the sunset. The bed was new and its covers matched the fabric of the low chairs, the skirted dressing-table and the window drapes filling and emptying softly in the evening breeze.

'There is another bedroom,' Brent informed Linette, pointing across the landing. 'And here,' he opened a door, 'is the bathroom.'

Linette gazed with astonishment at the gleaming shower fixture over the bath, the gracefully designed wash-basin, the floor-to-ceiling lemon-tinted tiles. It was, without doubt, the most modern part of the cottage.

'It was once a child's room,' Brent explained. He closed the door and motioned her down the stairs. Back in the living-room, he asked, 'Like the place?'

'It's beautiful, Brent. The architect's done wonders with it. When you showed me those 'before' pictures of it when it was a near-ruin, I thought the only thing that could be done was to demolish it.' She smiled. 'There's only one thing it lacks.'

'Which is——?'

'A tenant. Having furnished the place, I'd imagine your mother——'

'My mother is moving in with your uncle. He's agreed to share his cottage with her.'

## CHAPTER FIVE

'It's not true!' Her breath came quickly and she waited for the taunting smile telling her he was provoking her. His resolute look told her he had been perfectly serious. 'My uncle hasn't said anything to me. He wouldn't keep such a thing a secret.'

'He wanted to tell you, but I insisted that I should be the one.'

'It's my uncle's nature to be honest. No matter how much you might have insisted, he would have told me.'

'Don't forget,' was the cool response, 'that there was a third person involved—my mother. She agreed to fall in with my wishes.'

Linette felt defeated. She sought a seat, sinking down on to it. Then she remembered, and declared, 'There are only two bedrooms, Uncle Godfrey's and mine. So how——?' She frowned at the rug beneath her feet.

Its colours were russet and beige and blue. They formed themselves into a pleasing pattern before her bemused eyes at the very moment that the pattern of her future life fell starkly into place. The note attached to the bunch of flowers he had sent her read, *For Linette Kemp . . . who has no security of tenure whatsoever.*

Scrambling to her feet, she stormed, 'You've had your way, haven't you? You've been threatening me with eviction from the moment we met.'

'More a promise than a threat,' he corrected, 'and I always keep my promises.'

His tone was so reasonable she could have hit him. 'I'm being turned out of my home! It means nothing to you, Mr Napier, does it? You've got so many homes you could almost live in a different one each day.'

His eyebrows lifted, but he made no comment.

Linette sank down again. 'I don't believe it! Since that day your mother came round the cottage, she hasn't been near the place. So how could she discuss it with my uncle, how could she persuade him——' *Persuasion*, her uncle had said. She recalled his words. 'My niece is like me, honest and open . . . I'll have to do a lot of thinking . . .'

He must have done his thinking silently, without letting a word slip in her presence. But he must have seen Mrs Napier!

'Where did they meet to talk, Uncle Godfrey and your mother?'

He walked around, hands in his trouser pockets. 'In the George and Dragon, where else?'

'You mean your mother went to the village pub—where all my uncle's friends go?'

'Why not? Isn't that the best meeting place? The best leveller, where rich and poor, young and old, come together and chew over the news, both local and international?'

'And private matters about turning someone out of their home so that someone else can move in?'

'Don't sound so bitter, Linette.' His deep voice speaking her name was almost her undoing, rekindling the flame that he had only a few minutes ago almost extinguished. 'I thought you liked my mother?'

'I do, of course I do, but what's the use of that when I won't be sharing the cottage with her?' She touched her chin uncertainly. 'Uncle Godfrey and—and your mother, they'll be sharing it.'

'You think that's wrong? At their age? Come on, sweetheart,' he crouched in front of her, lifting her chin, 'they're old enough to know what they're about.'

Stunned, she saw his lips move towards hers. Without protest, she accepted the kiss, liking it in fact and holding her face up for more. His amber eyes were long-lashed and persuasive . . . *persuasion*. That was what this evening had been all about, his pretence at lovemaking, his apparent enjoyment of her company.

Twisting her face away, she shifted sideways. He straightened, looking down at her with a cool, level gaze. On her feet at once, she declared, 'I'm staying with my uncle. I know why he gave in. Without my help, he couldn't withstand the onslaught of the two of you getting at him.' Her eyes blazed into his. 'That's why you insisted on keeping the discussion a secret—so that my uncle had to stand alone, without me to back him up. Well, you've lost, Mr Napier.'

At the door, she flung back, 'Much as I like your mother, I'm not letting her into that cottage. It's like having a foot in the door. If I gave in now, next time it would be my uncle who's thrown out. I know your kind. You're not the great business executive for nothing. Well, you may have your subordinates and sycophants running round you at work, but we're not your employees. You can't pull the strings and make us dance and drop like puppets as you can them.'

'Oh, but I can, Miss Kemp,' the soft, menacing voice came after her, 'I can, and I will. That's a promise.'

The candle flame had gone out. He had pinched away its brightness between cruel fingers.

Wanting to cry because the world was falling about her ears, Linette ran all the way back to her uncle's cottage.

It was Godfrey's time for reading the morning paper. There were, he always said, better things to do with the daylight hours than reading lines of print.

When Linette burst in the door, pausing to catch her breath, he moved the paper down, then immediately lifted it again. It was almost as if he was hiding from her, probably, Linette concluded, because he did not want his concentration disturbed.

At that particular moment, it annoyed her that he was concentrating so hard. 'I'm sorry, Uncle Godfrey.' She had thrown a verbal missile at the newsprint and its impact had the desired effect. Her uncle surfaced, waiting patiently.

'I've just come from dining with Mr Napier.'

Godfrey nodded.

'I'm sorry,' Linette went on, 'about the way *they* forced you to keep it a secret.' Godfrey looked at her questioningly. 'I mean, the way they wouldn't let you tell me Mrs Napier wanted to move in and have my room. I know how honest you are. You would have told me, and I just can't forgive them for leaving you to fight them on your own.'

The layers of paper on his lap rustled. 'Yes, well, I——'

'But it's all right, Uncle. I'm not moving out. If I did, it would be you next.' She puzzled over his curious expression. 'You do understand, don't you?'

'Yes, Lin, I understand. I——'

'So I won't be deserting you. Anyway, I'd have nowhere to go, would I? I suppose I could go back to Mum and Dad, but it doesn't seem fair to wish myself on them again. They've got a life of their own to lead. So I'll be staying.' She stood in front of him, turning on her sweetest smile. 'Aren't you pleased?'

He gave a chuckle. 'Of course I am. I'm your uncle, aren't I? I wouldn't stand by and watch you made homeless.' The newspaper lifted again, more creased than before she had arrived.

The days went by. The children continued to come and go three mornings a week. On each alternate morning, Linette sold her uncle's produce. Too often for her liking, she found herself watching for a car, a large blue car. It did not come, nor did the owner or his mother.

Linette found herself beginning to fret. Even when she went to Leslie's house for the evening, helping to put Jenny to bed, she found she had brought the fretting with her. As they sat watching television, Leslie would sometimes pull her to his side and kiss her. There was a reason for her allowing him to do so—a purely selfish reason, she was forced to admit.

If she let Leslie kiss her, Linette's reasoning went, she

would be able to compare the feelings he aroused with
those stirred to life by Brent Napier's lovemaking. As the
evenings went by, she had to acknowledge that Leslie did
not arouse her at all.

The only time Linette felt she could relax was when
the children were around. From the moment they had
gone, until they came again, she found that a feeling of
anxiety persisted, and of longing—to see Brent Napier
again. It was this that worried her most, since it was plain
that he felt nothing for her, nothing at all.

Every evening her uncle continued to meet his friends in
the George and Dragon. He had told her that Mr Napier
had returned to London. It had come as a relief to know
that he was still in the country. He might well have gone
abroad, and if he had, there was no way of knowing when
he would return.

There had been no sign of his mother, who must,
Linette concluded, be in London with him. It would,
she thought one evening as she sat repairing her uncle's
jacket pocket, have been nice to have seen Mrs Napier
again. It had been very understanding of her to have
made no fuss when told, as she must have been, that
she could not, after all, move into Godfrey Barker's cottage.

A car drew to a halt outside. The slam of a door followed,
then came the firm tread of masculine footsteps. Linette
held her breath. Surely it wasn't—it wouldn't be Brent
Napier. He was in London, her uncle had told her. It was
plain the information had been out of date. The man was
here, knocking peremptorily, turning the handle and
walking in.

Now he was entering the room, coming to stand in front
of her, looking down first at her sewing, then into her
staring, unbelieving eyes. His half-smile tantalised, holding
secrets which she guessed she would never be told. His
lazy, entirely relaxed attitude irritated, since it spoke of a
power over her which no amount of opposition on her part
would alter.

'What do you want?' she queried irritably, dropping her eyes to her sewing.

'What a welcome from the girl I've raced back from London to see!'

'Why should I welcome you? Ever since I've known you, you've done your darnedest to evict me from my home.'

'But it isn't your home, is it?'

His words held a note of menace which had Linette's head jerking up. 'Haven't I told you—only the other night, in fact——'

'That you've nowhere else to go,' he took her up. His fists found his hips and Linette's gaze was drawn to the strong muscularity of his legs beneath the brown, well-worn slacks. His shirt-sleeves were rolled, the buttons partly opened. Over his shoulders was draped a lightweight zipped jacket.

'Well, we're going somewhere now. Put aside that sewing and get a jacket.'

Her hands moved in obedience to his command since her mind was too preoccupied with what he had said to stop them. 'Going where? Not out to dinner, thank you. I had my evening meal with Uncle Godfrey.'

'For a drive, maybe a drink.' He watched her look down at herself. 'Those jeans will do, and that striped thing you're wearing.' He pushed a finger into the neckline of her blouse and she shivered involuntarily at the touch of him. 'Cold?' he asked. 'Get a jacket.'

'I don't need one.'

'It gets cool in the evening. Go and get one.' She defied his insistence and stood her ground. His shoulders lifted. 'If you start sneezing, don't blame me.'

'My hair.' Her hands lifted. 'It needs combing.'

'It's fine. These are delaying tactics.'

'I'm going to comb it. I'm not going anywhere looking scruffy with you.'

He caught her shoulder and pulled her nearer, at the same time extracting a comb from his pocket. 'Come here.' His hand spread under her chin, while his other ran his comb through her brown curls. All the while she gazed up at him, and at that moment, did not care if he saw all her feeling in her eyes.

His eyes slid down, caught her stare with his and the moment held. There was a rocking sensation inside her, as if they were standing on a pinnacle locked in a timeless embrace. If they moved, they would plunge, still clinging, into eternity.

It was Brent who recovered first, snapping the thread and breaking the dream. Only when he released her shoulder did Linette realise how hard he had been gripping her. Had he experienced the same sensation, but recovered his balance, refusing to fall?

I can't imagine, Linette thought as reality returned, Brent Napier falling anywhere or for anything, most certainly not in love, least of all with me.

'It makes no difference,' he was saying, 'whether it's combed or not. It's as unruly now as it was before.'

'Thank you very much,' she responded sarcastically. 'Wherever it is you're going, you'd better go there without me.'

His answer was to put his arm across her shoulders, grip the soft flesh of her upper arm and propel her towards the door. Outside, he unlocked the car.

'Get in,' he ordered, waiting while she obeyed.

Mutinously she took her seat, watching as he eased himself behind the steering wheel. 'Do you talk to your underlings like that?' she wanted to know. 'If you do, it's a wonder you haven't had a string of strikes on your hands!'

'None of my employees, however senior, talks to me the way you do.' He pulled away from the kerb and drove to the junction with the main road. 'Therefore I can talk to them reasonably, knowing I'll get a balanced reply. There's no need for the arguments and squabbles which you seem to thrive on.'

'I don't argue or quarrel with anyone except you. No one else is determined to throw me out on the streets.'

Brent smiled at the road ahead. 'How you do turn on the sentiment!'

Linette uttered an exasperated, 'Oh!' and stared at the passing scenery. They drove through the small and ancient town of Chipping Camden, the stone of its buildings catching the remaining light and despite the approaching darkness, reflecting it back.

The houses and buildings of the town, her uncle had told her, dated from every century since the fourteenth, but the varied styles blended excellently. Through the years, the same Cotswold stone had been used in their construction.

A short distance outside the town, Brent turned off the road and bumped into the car park of a village inn. Entering. Linette gazed around, but saw no one she knew. Her uncle's friends did not usually venture this far, and her own acquaintances were small in number.

Brent led her to a two-seater banquette half hidden in a corner. Asking her for her choice of drink, he went to the counter. From a safe distance Linette watched him, noting how his commanding air helped him catch the eye of the bartender, despite the fact that others crowded round.

His jacket was on the seat beside her and her hand strayed to rest on it. Her mind played a moment's game of makebelieve, that she, like the jacket, belonged to him. The urge to lift it to her cheek was so strong she had to fight to gain control, then looked down to see that her clenched hand had left a moist imprint.

As she tried to stroke the creases away, she became aware that Brent stood watching her, his lips curved sardonically. 'Imagining I'm inside it and that you're stroking me?'

Her cheeks glowed pink and she hoped he would think the red-tinted lighting around the walls was the cause. 'I—you——' With what she hoped was a gesture of distaste, she pushed the garment away.

He laughed at her confusion and lowered the drinks to the knee-high table. Hanging his jacket on a nearby coat-stand, he returned to his seat. Its lack of width had brought him uncomfortably close, so that his thigh pressed against hers.

Seizing his glass and lifting it, he stole a look at her. She saw the quizzical expression, as if he was as aware of the feel of her as she of him, and that he intended doing nothing about it. Fascinated, Linette watched the huge swallows pass down his strong throat. In no more than a few moments, the glass was half empty. Lowering it to the table, he turned again and caught her look of wonder. His head went back in laughter and his hand found a resting place on her jean-clad thigh.

The sensation of excitement was immediate, spreading from her leg to invade her body. As her own hand lowered to push his away, her eye saw again the dark hairs on his arm, while those around his wrist were confined by the stretch-strap of his watch. It was then that her hand rebelled against her brain's instruction. Instead of pushing, it pressed, and his palm and fingers must have detected the warmth of her skin which their pressure brought about.

With her head on one side, Linette picked up his smile, tossing it back. Pleased with herself for having turned the tables on him, she remarked, 'Now you'll have to ask for your hand back. You had no right to put it there in the first place.'

'I noticed you didn't object when I did.' With a spurt of anger at the truth of his words, her fingers tightened around his. A shoulder lifted. 'I'm content if you are.' The glass went to his mouth and this time he emptied it, while her glass stood untouched.

He looked at the bar. 'I'll get another,' he informed her, and was away across to the counter before she knew his hand had gone from her.

To conceal her annoyance that he had won that skirmish, Linette swallowed some of her drink. The entrance door opened, letting in a current of cold air, and a middle-aged couple entered. The man nodded to her, while the woman smiled. To Linette, she was vaguely familiar.

The moment she recalled that she had once or twice

served the woman with fruit and vegetables from her uncle's stall, she heard her voice asking, 'Here all alone, Miss Kemp?'

'No, I'm not alone——' If only she could remember the woman's name! It did not matter, as the woman's attention was already on Brent's impressive figure at the counter. 'Isn't that gentleman the owner of Wealden Grange? Oh, and your uncle's cottage, of course. Rumour says, Miss Kemp,' the woman was whispering loudly, 'he had the bailiffs get to work on your uncle's place, but he called them off. No one knows why.'

Brent appeared, standing by the table.

'Oh, I'm so sorry, Miss Kemp,' the woman said. 'I didn't realise he was with you.' She laughed selfconsciously, 'Getting friendly with him, are you? Well, that's as good a way as any to persuade him to let you stay!' With a laugh and a wave, she went on her way.

'Who is that woman?' Brent lowered himself to the seat and took a long drink. The action did not hide from Linette the way his jaw had hardened.

She shrugged. 'A customer of my uncle's. I've served her once or twice.'

'Does she live in the village?' Linette nodded. 'Which is how she hears so-called rumours.'

He glanced over the heads of the customers, appearing to note how the woman chattered and gestured towards the corner where he sat with Linette.

'There'll be more rumours now,' he said, and met her questioning gaze. 'About you and me. What, everyone will wonder, are you doing to *persuade* me to let you and your uncle stay?' He smiled sardonically. 'Well, Miss Kemp, what are you intending to do to make me change my mind?'

He looked down at her with hooded eyes. Once again, his hand rested where it had been before. The same unnerving sensations chased up and down her spine, but this time she forced her hand to push his away. Brent was unperturbed by her gesture.

His arm went round her shoulders, while his free hand lifted her chin. 'Shall we give them something to gossip about?' He moved his hand, flicked at a stray curl, then, taking her completely by surprise, took her pouting lips in a swift kiss.

His fingers pinching her chin prevented her from turning her head in visible protest. 'Will you stop it?' she muttered between her teeth. He laughed at her anger and let her go.

'Anyway,' she rubbed trembling fingers up and down the stem of her glass, 'they've got it all wrong. You're the one who's supposed to be doing the persuading. Working on me, wasn't it, to get me to accept your mother's presence in Uncle Godfrey's cottage?'

'It's something you're going to have to accept eventually.' He made as if to rise. 'Drink up. We're going.' He emptied his glass, then replaced it with a thump on the table. He disengaged his jacket from under other garments and pulled it on.

As they left behind them the noise and clatter of the inn, Linette asked, hurrying to keep pace with Brent's long strides, 'What did you mean, I'll have to accept it?'

There was no reply. They did not speak again until the car drew up outside her uncle's cottage, and even then Linette received no answer. Brent erupted from the car, slamming the door, then going round to lock the passenger's side. He seemed angry, and Linette did not relish the thought of entertaining him alone. 'My uncle will be back,' she said, more in hope than expectation.

'I doubt it. The pubs don't close for well over half an hour.'

As usual, he was right. The place was empty, except that Brent's compelling personality seemed to fill it. He removed his jacket and tossed it on to a chair.

'You want an answer to your question?' he asked, pushing his hands into his pockets.

There was a strange weakness in Linette's legs at the thought of what might be coming. She sank on to the couch, hoping her tension did not show. 'I'm ready,' she declared, with a bravado she did not feel, 'for anything!'

His eyebrow quirked at the double meaning, but he was plainly in no mood for levity. 'My mother is moving into this cottage,' he stated, taking up a position immediately in front of her. 'Your uncle has agreed. It's all arranged.'

*Ready for anything*, she had quipped. But not for this! The colour left her cheeks and her hand went, in an uncertain, childlike action, to her mouth.

'Uncle Godfrey agreed? I don't believe it!' Unmoved, Brent looked down into her panic-stricken eyes. 'If he did, it must have been under duress, and you don't have to keep any promise made under duress. If you forced agreement from him——'

'No force—verbal or arm-twisting, metaphorically, of course—was needed. He seemed pleased with the idea.'

Stunned, she confronted him, only to find he was disconcertingly nearer. 'Uncle Godfrey pleased? It's not true! He must have known I'd have to move out—unless,' the terrible thought struck her, 'he's being made to move out, too?'

'He's staying.'

'Then I'll be the one . . .' She gripped her throat, her eyes pleading. 'Brent, please don't make me move out. I've got nowhere——'

'I'm offering you the cottage on the estate.'

Her eyes opened wide in accusation. 'So that's what it was all about when we dined there! To soften my attitude towards it.'

'You liked it from the moment you went in. Even before that, when you saw the photograph.'

'I can't live there. I haven't got a job, so I couldn't pay rent.'

'It will be rent-free.'

'Philanthropy,' she sneered, 'from you? I can't imagine you giving anything without demanding something in return.'

'Thanks for the compliment,' he answered expressionlessly. 'Your gratitude touches my heart.'

'Gratitude? When I'm being deprived of my home, and all the familiar things about this place I've grown to love? Why should I show any gratitude for that?' She went to the window, stared out, came back. 'You can keep your cottage. You'd have to get the bailiffs back to get me out of here!'

The challenge was in her eyes, the lift of her head, her whole tense body. The suppressed anger in the eyes that met hers made her waver inside, but she refused to acknowledge any feeling of fear. All right, so he was a strong, powerful man, both in physique and mind, but she could be strong, too, couldn't she?

It was even possible, she discovered, to summon a smile. It brought no answering smile from him. Instead there was an ominous tightening of his mouth, a glitter in his eyes. His hands whipped from his pockets and fastened on to her shoulders. There was a leashed anger about him which was all the more frightening for the restraint he was imposing on it.

Certain that he was about to shake her—and if he did his mercy would be nil—Linette made her limbs go rigid. Unexpectedly, his hands left her and she swayed at the abrupt withdrawal of support.

'So be it,' he said tautly, and walked out.

Half an hour later there was the sound of a key in the lock. There were voices outside, from which Linette deduced that her uncle had brought a friend back with him.

'Still up, Lin?' Godfrey greeted his niece.

'Just going to bed, Uncle. Evening, Mr Ellington.' Linette smiled, and the visitor nodded pleasantly, but she still could not bring herself to dissociate the man with the time he had almost turned traitor on her uncle, at Brent Napier's request, and tried to turn them out of the cottage.

It seemed, however, that her uncle had forgiven and forgotten. 'Sit down, Tom,' the round-faced, well-built man complied, 'and I'll make us a cup of tea.'

'Shall I do it, Uncle Godfrey?'

'No, you go up, lass.'

'Uncle——' He turned to her and she wondered if she
had imagined the quick, selfconscious expression in his
eyes. She looked at the visitor and decided against confronting her uncle with the allegation which Brent Napier
had made that he had agreed to Mrs Napier moving in.
She shook her head. 'It's okay, Uncle. It can wait until
morning.'

An hour later, as she listened to her uncle showing out
his visitor, then locking up, Linette wished she could put
Brent Napier's face out of her mind.

At last she fell into a deep sleep, with dreams so vivid
she could smell, feel and hear them. There was a voice
speaking quietly, although she could not distinguish the
words. Then she was floating, and Brent's arms were
carrying her. For support she clung to his neck and her
face snuggled against him. She could feel the roughness of
the hair springing from his chest, smell the musky maleness,
and in her dream, she took immense comfort from the
strength of him.

Her hand moved exploringly down his firm cheek, the
pads of her fingers rubbing against the bristles which,
even in the dream, were sharp. There were jerky movements now, and no more floating. Someone was truly
carrying her. Her eyes flew open and, blinking in the bright
light over the staircase, she perceived the outline of a face
which, over the weeks, had grown heartbreakingly
familiar.

'Brent?' He came to a stop. 'What's happening? Is the
place on fire? Where's Uncle Godfrey?'

'There's no fire, and your uncle is safely in his bed. And,
before you ask, I'm here with his consent.'

Her fingers clutched at his shirt collar. 'What do you
mean, with his consent? I was asleep, and you woke me
up. Why, Brent, why?'

He started walking again without answering her question. She stared at all the familiar things, which, to her

sleep-hazed eyes, appeared to be wrapped around in mist. Feeling separate and apart, as if the dream she believed she was dreaming was continuing, she watched as he approached the front door. It was then that reality hit her.

'You're not taking me out of here! Where are we going? Uncle—Uncle Godfrey . . .'

'I'm sorry, Lin dear. This was the only way.'

Her body twisted in Brent's arms as she craned to look up the stairs at her uncle. 'Why are you sorry? What about? What only way?'

Her uncle shook his head slowly and walked wearily back to his room, calling out, 'I'll lock up, Mr Napier.'

'I'm not going out there with you. Look,' she tugged at the short skirt of her thin nightdress, 'I'll be cold, I'll freeze!'

'There's a rug in the car.'

'What car?' Her voice rose. 'Why won't somebody tell me?'

'My car.' Brent strode across and dumped her squirming body in the rear seat, wrapping a blanket around her. Then he stood, hand against the car roof. In the beam from the central light, Linette could see the resolution in his face. 'I'm taking you to the cottage.'

'I'm not going there! I told you "no"!'

He slammed the door, flung himself into the driving seat and fired the engine. The car swung round the corner, sped along the road towards his house and bumped through the opened gates. Turning left, he proceeded more slowly along the narrow road to the cottage.

It was as if it had all been prepared in advance. Lights were on inside the cottage, curtains were pulled across the windows. Linette, who had struggled into a sitting position, decided to make a quick getaway and swung the car door wide. A step outside and she would be on her way to freedom.

It was then that she realised there was not the slightest possibility of escape. Her feet were bare. If she tried escaping, she would be unable to bear the pain of the pebbles

and the rough surfaces of pathways and road. By now,
Brent had reached across to where she had shifted away
from him. He caught her arm and pulled, but she resisted
and cried out at the pain.

'Just relax,' he advised, 'then you won't get hurt. Come
what may, you're going in there,' his head indicated the
subdued glow behind the drawn curtains, 'and what's
more, you're staying there.'

With a determined stride into the car he scooped her
up, blanket still round her, and eased her out and into his
arms. 'Put me down!' Linette shrieked, kicking her legs.
He dealt easily with her struggles.

'All in good time,' was his measured answer.

The cottage door was unlocked and he swung her inside,
making for the stairs. They were half-way up before she
had time to take a breath to protest.

'I'm not staying,' she declared, 'you can't make me!'

They were at the top now and she twisted to clutch at
his shoulders. Beneath the thin cotton of his shirt she could
feel the muscles tautened by his hold on her. Undeterred,
she tried to shake him, only succeeding in levering herself
backwards and forwards.

Now they had entered the bedroom he had shown her
on their first visit. Brent switched on the light, then
swung her legs to the floor. The moment he did so the
blanket fell away. Without its folds to hinder her,
Linette made a dive for the entrance. But even as she
fled, she realised it was an empty gesture. She would
have got no farther than the head of the stairs before
he had caught her up.

Belatedly, she came to a stop, returning despondently,
hands to her cheeks. Brent had not moved a step, so confident was he that she could not get away. I'll wait, she
thought, endeavouring to rally her spirits, I'll wait until he
leaves, then I'll risk injuring my feet and walk back home.

'How long will it be,' she asked, tracing imaginary pat-
terns with her toe on the plain beige carpet, 'before your
mother moves in?' Her head lifted questioningly, as she

pretended to have accepted the situation, but she received no answer.

His eyes were moving with masculine interest over her nightdress. Linette remembered that it was possible to see through the thin material. She reached out for the blanket, but he was there first, tossing it aside. All she could do now was to wrap her hands around her, but it proved a useless gesture.

He looked down at her, his eyes in shadow, and she began to shiver. 'I'm c-cold,' she complained, but knew it was more with shock than chill. He did not seem to have heard. One by one, her hands were prised from around her own waist and held firmly in his.

Lingeringly, his eyes wandered over the slim, jutting outline of her body. 'I wonder,' he said, 'if you realise how attractive you are? But,' his eyelids half closed, 'your boy-friend must have told you many times.'

'If you mean Leslie Dickins,' she hit back, 'he's never seen me like this.'

'Stupid of me,' he drawled, 'to have made such an ele-mentary mistake. By now he would almost certainly have undressed you completely.' A stride brought him nearer. Releasing her hands, he stooped to the hem of the gown, but guessing his intention, Linette twisted away and stood by the door.

'If you so much as touch me,' she breathed, 'I'll get you for assault!'

'You do that,' he flung back, 'and I'll have you out of here and your uncle out of there,' his stabbing finger indicated the other cottage, 'faster than you can say "please, don't"!'

He had got her and she knew it. So did he. Head slightly down, he approached and she shrank back against the solid and ancient wood of the door. 'If you so much as touch me,' she repeated shakily. 'I'll—I'll——' She would what? He would laugh in her face if she made the same threat as before.

'You'll what?' He folded his arms and waited with jeering amusement.

'As soon as you leave, I'll run back home.' She could have bitten her tongue for telling him her secret.

'Thanks for letting me know,' he said, smiling without mirth, 'but you wouldn't get far with bare feet.' This, she told herself miserably, she was already aware of. 'And anyway,' he continued with relish, 'I can run faster than you.'

A terrible weariness hit her and her body drooped. The shaking began again. 'All I want to do,' she whispered, half to herself, 'is go to sleep.'

Strong hands slid behind and beneath her, lifting and carrying her. The gentleness had her arms holding fast to him and she turned her cheek to his chest. Beside the double bed, on which the covers had been drawn back, he paused, and the gentleness was gone. His hands which were spread over her thighs and shoulders tightened their hold.

His face was a mere breathing distance from hers. 'How do I know,' he demanded, 'that all this isn't play-acting? That the moment my back's turned you won't make your stupid attempt to run?'

His distrust caused her momentarily to rally. 'I want to rest, and sleep. I told you, didn't I?'

Her show of temper was her undoing. She saw from his glinting eyes that his suspicion had deepened. He dropped her on to the bed, stripped off his shirt and slacks, leaving only his underpants. He switched off the light and threw himself beside her, covering them both with the quilt. He gathered her into the strength of his arms and she was hauled against him in an embrace of steel.

'Now try to get away from me,' he mouthed against her ear.

Despite the warmth of him which wrapped itself around her, the shaking returned. Now, it was not the cold air which was causing it, but the hard nearness of him running the length and breadth of her.

'Be still,' he whispered, 'settle down and have the sleep you want.'

'I just c-can't,' Linette whispered back, her hand lifting and grasping at his chest hair, 'it's impossible.'

It was impossible, she told herself, not only to sleep, but to pretend Brent was not there. How could she relax when the solid, muscle-hard feel of him against her was causing tiny pulses to beat all over her body? In no way could she give a sign of the arousal of her very feminine responses.

That, she knew intuitively, would act as the spark with which to set his desires alight, then where would she be? In the middle of a disastrous affair with him—disastrous because there could be no question of his ever falling in love with her, whereas she was more than halfway in love with him already.

Oh yes, she admitted, sighing with peace and pleasure, as his stroking hand in the darkness passed over her hair, his fingers running down her cheek to rest in the hollows of her throat. His hand was turning her head, his lips resting on her eyes, her chin and finally securing her mouth.

With her head moving negatively but uselessly against the pillows, she tried to mouth 'no', but his lips, becoming every moment more audacious, prevented all protest. His hand had insinuated itself between her nightdress and her body. His feathering palm excited her skin all the way up to her breasts, holding and stroking them, bringing her responses near to fever-pitch.

Her lips were parted now and she felt the probe of his lips against her teeth. Her resistance had crumbled and her fingers made their imprint on the hard flesh of his back.

It wouldn't be long, she thought hazily, before she was faced with the ultimate decision. His desire was strong against her and she longed to let him master her entirely. Yet what would it mean without love?

'Is it "yes", sweetheart?' he asked. 'Are you telling me not to hold back but make you mine? Tell me, for pity's sake, tell me!'

'No, no,' she moaned, in anguish at having to refuse, not only to satisfy his needs, but also to alleviate the aching pain of her own disappointed passion. But she could not let this man take over her body and her life. That was what it would be, when his sole intention was to dislodge her from everything else she held dear. 'I'm not telling you to do anything.' Even at that moment, she sensed the first signs of his drawing away. Somehow she must justify her refusal.

She spoke out as the truth hit her. 'You started it,' she accused. 'You got into bed beside me.' Brent lay on his back, arm uplifted to rest on his forehead. She gazed at his sculpted profile. 'What—what you thought was encouragement was my natural response to you beside me.'

'Okay,' he growled, 'you've made your point.' He rolled off the bed, switching on the bedside lamp.

'Where are you going, Brent?'

'Back to my home.' He dressed, fastening his shirt buttons. His eyes flicked over her as she lay on the bed. 'You should have told me you were that sort.'

'What sort, Brent?' She could not help the anxious appeal in her eyes, the wavering note in her voice.

'The sort who cheats. The kind who gets a man where she wants him and then, at the last minute, puts up the barriers.'

'I didn't want you there, Brent.' Why was she defending herself, when she should be accusing him of forcing himself on her? 'I didn't invite you.'

'Didn't you?' he sneered, and she knew he was right. Of course she had wanted him there. What was more, she had *wanted* him—but with love, with love . . .

He opened the door. How could she detain him, she wondered, yet knowing she would be playing with fire? Lifting herself on to her elbow, she threatened, 'If you go, I'll run back home.'

'Go home, if that's what you want,' he retaliated, and slammed his way out of the cottage.

He had called her bluff. He knew, as she knew, that she would stay until morning.

When Linette awoke, there was a feeling inside her that she had slept late. Her watch had been left behind at her uncle's cottage and there was no clock in the room to tell her the time.

If her empty stomach was anything to go by, she thought it must be past mid-morning. Pulling a sheet from the bed and tying it round her sarong-style, she went downstairs. A search in the kitchen produced milk and bread from the refrigerator. Other food was there, too. There was a smart new cooking stove which, she judged, remembering the meal which Mary had cooked the evening Brent had taken her there to dine, worked well.

In the kitchen cupboard there were saucepans and a frying pan, cups, saucers, everything, in fact, a home would need. But whose home? Did it mean that Brent had really intended it to be hers? And had he honestly believed she would have agreed to stay there after his abduction of her—which was what the snatching of her from her bed had amounted to.

As she sat at the breakfast counter which had been built along one wall, and ate with relish the egg on toast she had cooked herself, she remembered that there had even been towels and soap in the bathroom when she had washed that morning.

From somewhere a clock chimed, light and sweet on the quiet morning air. Linette counted—twelve o'clock? Gathering her dishes and carrying them to the sink, she dashed into the smaller of the two living-rooms. There it was, on the mantelpiece, all gilt and glass and swaying pendulum. The clock must be an antique, she reasoned, admiring it, but did it keep good time?

In the distance, the clock on the village church tower struck twelve, proving beyond doubt that the small clock was correct. Despite the tumult in which Brent had left her emotions, she had slept, and slept deeply, for hours after his departure.

Hurriedly she washed the dishes, finding the water from the hot tap living up to its name, as indeed it had upstairs in the bathroom. Leaving the dishes to drain, she rearranged the sheet around her like a cloak and went to the door.

The prospect of walking barefoot along that gravel path was daunting. After that came the road from the gates of the estate ... Linette squared her shoulders. 'It's no use hesitating,' she said aloud, 'there's no other way.'

Walking on grass for as long as possible, she had in the end to negotiate the pebbles. Each step was a miniature torture, and every three or four paces she was forced to pause and brush away the pebbles which clung to the underside of her feet. There were even tears in her eyes, she discovered, as she neared the entrance gates.

Hoping the small walk-through gate was not locked, she tried the handle. It gave, and she sighed with relief. It seemed that Brent had meant what he said when he had told her so unpleasantly to go back home. Well, for once she would do as he told her, and with pleasure, she thought rebelliously, closing the door behind her.

The walk along the road was little better. Even over the slightly smoother surface, small stones were scattered. The grass path alongside soon dipped down into a ditch. This forced her back on to a rough walking surface. Arriving at the junction of the private road with the main road which ran past her uncle's cottage, she paused again, glancing right and left, hoping there was no one around to see her strange style of dress.

Something made her turn. A man, tall and lean, stood watching her. His arms were folded across his chest, his feet belligerently apart. Linette jerked at the sheet to wrap it more firmly around her, then stared intently at the man to see if he was laughing.

His face was unsmiling and as intimidating as his stance. How long had he been watching? Something told her it must have been from the moment she had left the cottage. If so, why hadn't he offered her a lift? Flinging an angry look at him, she continued on her way, limping awkwardly.

By the time she entered her uncle's front door, it seemed

as if she had been walking for days. There was a pleasant aroma of food, which could only mean that her uncle had been forced to cook his own lunch. It was something she had never known him do before, having assumed he did not even know how to use the cooker.

'Uncle?' she called, her uncertainty showing in her voice. 'It's me. I'm back. I refused to stay at the other cottage, so——'

'Linette!' Godfrey appeared from the kitchen, fork in his hand. He was dabbing at his mouth with his napkin. 'What are you doing here? And dressed like that . . .' Linette looked down at herself.

'Oh, my goodness,' a woman's voice exclaimed, 'whatever has happened?'

Linette looked into the anxious eyes of Brent Napier's mother. 'Mrs Napier,' she exclaimed, aghast, looking from the visitor to her uncle, 'why are you here?' Her uncle's meal—had Mrs Napier cooked it? 'What's going on?'

There was a movement behind her and Linette swung round. Brent stood in the doorway, a twisted smile on his face. 'Linette, meet your uncle's new sub-tenant. Mother, Linette. Linette——'

'Now I know,' the object of his mockery hit out at him, 'why you didn't answer when I asked you when your mother was moving in.'

Brent strolled to stand beside her. 'As I remember it,' he drawled, 'at the time you were not particularly interested in the answer.'

Turning away, Linette felt the colour stain her cheeks. He had, she recalled, been staring in excruciating detail at the parts of her which showed through the material of her nightdress.

'How—how long are you staying, Mrs Napier?' she asked.

Her uncle answered. 'For as long as she wants, Lin,' he explained with a touch of hesitancy.

'But, Uncle Godfrey, there are only two bedrooms here—yours and mine.'

'Not now, dear, not now,' he answered, plainly hoping by his tone to placate her. He ran a finger round his shirt collar. 'You see, your room belongs to Mrs Napier now. It's all arranged. From now on, you'll be living in Mr Napier's cottage.'

# CHAPTER SIX

'UNCLE GODFREY,' Linette pleaded, 'this is my home. How could you have agreed to allow me to be—to be evicted?'

'It was out of my hands, Lin. I'm just the tenant, you know that. And anyway, I knew you were being given another place—a whole cottage, more room . . .'

'Well,' she swung to face Brent, pulling the sheet more tightly around her, 'the wonderful, thoughtful landlord can keep his cottage! I'm not living there. I'm not living anywhere.' A feeling of desolation came from nowhere. She turned miserably to the wall, put her arm up and rested her head against it. Her slim frame was shaken by sobs.

'Oh, my dear!' Mrs Napier exclaimed, moving across and putting her arm around the shaking shoulders. 'If I'd known how deeply you felt about this . . . But I thought you'd love that little cottage Brent's offered you. He furnished it with such care, he spared no expense to make it comfortable.'

'I still don't want it,' Linette mumbled, her voice thick.

'Mother,' a man spoke softly, and there were a series of movements, only partly heard over the short, sobbing breaths of the grief-stricken figure.

'Brent, she's upset. Be gentle.'

'He couldn't be if he tried,' the tear-filled voice interposed. When another, more muscular arm came round her, she tried to shake it off, but it was a feeble attempt. She was turned to be received in an enveloping embrace, and she gave herself up to the solid comfort of it.

It was all she wanted, really, she told herself, pressing her forehead against the deeply-breathing chest. Security, stability, a man whose mental strength matched his physical powers, a man to laugh with and love with—especially love. With a will of its own, her cheek turned and burrowed into the reassurance of him. This man, she told herself, only this man would do, no other, ever.

'Brent,' Mrs Napier spoke from the kitchen doorway, then, in a very different tone, '*Brent?*'

He moved as if his head was shaking dismissively. 'Linette,' he asked at last, 'your clothes—what do you need?'

Linette moved away, more composed now, seeking in vain for a handkerchief. Brent pulled out a clean, folded one from his pocket. His shirt was bronze-coloured, matching his eyes, and his manner was as relaxed as his chosen style of dress. It was the weekend, after all, Linette reminded herself.

With the handkerchief, she scrubbed at her eyes. 'Can't I at least go upstairs and get my own things?' she queried, frowning.

'Why not, my dear?' Mrs Napier replied for her son. 'Your belongings have all been carefully packed, including your miniatures which I myself wrapped individually in newspaper. I did leave a pair of jeans and a blouse and some other things in the cupboard and drawers.'

'That was kind of you, Mrs Napier,' Linette answered, her manner subdued.

'Not at all. Go up and help yourself.'

'Can you manage?' Brent's voice as she limped up the stairs was sincere but neutral.

'Perfectly well, thank you.' Linette hoped her distant tone would make him forget the way she had clung to him a few minutes ago, but his slight smile told her that nothing would do that. Well, she asked herself wearily, would she ever forget the feel of him as he had lain beside her last night or the way she longed to give herself, body and soul, into his keeping?

Finding her clothes and dressing in them, she reflected that he already had more than enough power over her. She experienced a surge of thankfulness that she had not, in fact, agreed to let him love her fully.

Having finished dressing and trying to hide the after-effects of the tears, she washed her feet and was attempting to inspect their undersides when Brent walked in. He carried a bowl of water and a roll of cotton wool.

'I didn't ask for your help,' she greeted him coolly.

He ignored her petulance. 'Sit on the bed.'

It was obviously useless to argue with a man who spoke so authoritatively, so Linette flopped down, but with a show of reluctance. He held her feet, one by one, with a gentleness she had experienced fleetingly from him in the early hours.

It was impossible to deny the pleasure it gave her to feel the touch of him again. She cursed the perverseness of her emotions in causing her to plunge headlong into loving a man who felt nothing for her but annoyance at her refusal to do as he wanted, yet who manipulated her with such ease and without care for her wishes, into doing just those things.

Her eyes studied the top of his head, intrigued by the way his hair seemed to be parted against his own in-clinations, but remained smooth and tidy. Only this man, she thought with a secret smile, would be able to assert authority over such a wayward thing as wrongly-parted hair!

His finger ran lightly down the centre of her left sole, making the toes curl. 'No damage here, but this one,' he picked up her right foot, 'has a thorn embedded.' He asked for tweezers.

'In the bathroom cabinet,' she directed him.

He was soon back and probing at the thorn. She winced and he apologised, putting his hand on her ankle in a soothing action.

'I'm trying not to hurt you, but it's gone in deeply, so I may not be able to avoid it. Grit your teeth,' he advised.

Linette so liked the feel of his hand where it was that she wanted to clamp it there. Instead, she gritted her teeth as he had advised. The knowledge came to her that she would probably be gritting her teeth all through her life, whenever, in fact, she thought about the man. This, judging by the way he seemed constantly to be in her thoughts in the present, would be tormentingly often in the days and years to come.

'There was no need for you to do this,' she commented, feeling the need to break the silence. 'My uncle would have come, or your mother.'

'They offered, but I preferred to do it myself. After all,' her foot received the benefit of his reminiscent smile, 'when you've kissed a girl as much as I've kissed you, not to mention holding her in your arms, you get the feeling there must be something between us.'

'Yes,' she answered promptly, hoping to annoy him, 'desire pure and simple on your side, and a wish to pacify the landlord on mine. Oh, that hurt!'

Brent held up the offending thorn which was still caught between the tweezers' blades. 'Pure coincidence that it came out at that moment,' he grinned. Putting aside the antiseptic and other utensils, he stood in front of her, caught her hands and pulled her into his arms.

Standing as she was, barefoot and on tiptoe, he seemed as tall as a giant. Her head tipped back to look into his face. It held a taunting smile and she knew it was only a matter of seconds before his head lowered, his mouth meeting hers.

Perversely she turned away, but his hand on her cheek forced her to face him again. He took his kiss, then another, while her hands rested obstinately on his shoulders. She would not let them creep round his neck.

He had just commented on how many times they had kissed. If she continued to allow him to do so whenever he wished, who knew where that would lead? And all the time she would know she meant nothing but a diversion to him. Hadn't she seen him with that woman, the way he had looked at her and she at him?

All the time the thoughts had been passing through her head, his lips had been playing havoc with hers, the pressure making them throb yet offer themselves for more. His hands had not been idle, skimming the shape of her, making themselves familiar with her hips, her waist and lingering at last on the warm femininity of her breasts.

There was a sound in the half-open doorway. Brent was the first to break contact. Without it, Linette found herself drooping, like a climbing plant whose support had been removed.

Mrs Napier watched, a little worried, as her son ran smoothing hands over his hair and Linette dropped back to her seat on the bed. 'Brent? Linette? There's some food left over if you'd like it.'

'No, thanks, Mother. I've eaten. Mary cooked me a snack. I expect Linette would like something?'

Linette changed the negative shake of her head to a nod. It was a long time since she had had breakfast. 'Thank you, Mrs Napier,' she answered quietly. 'I'll be down soon.'

'That's good, dear. Brent?' There was a firm invitation in the maternal voice.

'Your feet should be fine now, Linette,' said Brent as he left her, his tone clipped. 'Look after them.'

The door did not shut completely behind him. Voices came from another room—her uncle's bedroom, Linette assumed, but her uncle was not there. It was impossible to close her ears to the words that were being exchanged.

'Call me an interfering parent if you like, Brent, but please—please don't play with that sweet girl's emotions. Where women are concerned, dear, you've hardly got a clean slate——'

'Will you let me be, Mother?' was the angry reply. 'I'm a grown man. I know exactly what I'm doing.'

It seemed his mother did not believe him. 'She's hardly your taste, Brent, now is she? By no stretch of the imagination could you call her the cool, sophisticated type you seem to favour—although why, heaven knows. She's the sweetest, most gentle——'

'When I want your verbal testimonial on one Linette Kemp, if I should ever contemplate employing—or even marrying—the girl, I'll ask for it. Until then——'

Linette propelled herself outside and flung open the door of her uncle's bedroom. She took a few steps inside and declared angrily,

'Thank you for standing up for me, Mrs Napier, but I don't care a damn what your son thinks of me. If I could break his heart, I would, but as I've discovered, he hasn't got a heart to break.'

It was imperative to pause for breath and she saw Brent's ice-cold eyes were on her. They did not cool the heat of her fury. She'd get even with him somehow, she vowed, even if it meant telling an untruth to do so.

'I've got a boy-friend of my own, as your son knows.' She tried a too-sweet smile, but it crystallised and hardened. 'It's Leslie Dickins. He's got a child, but he's divorcing his wife. We're friends—good friends.' She threw Brent a burning look. Let him take that how he likes, she thought uncaringly. 'So there's no need to worry about my feelings, Mrs Napier, no need at all.'

Running from them, she sought the sanctuary of the bedroom which used to be hers and flung herself sideways on to the bed. Her fists pounded its softness, her forehead pressed against the covers. The tears were there, fighting to be released, but on no account would she let them come.

Soon she calmed herself down, pangs of hunger having intruded upon her distress. When she appeared in the kitchen, her uncle had returned to his garden and Brent had gone. Mrs Napier was at the sink washing the dishes.

At once she stopped, peeling off her rubber gloves and serving the still-warm food to Linette. 'There, dear, you'll enjoy that. I cooked it myself.'

Linette's smile was a little wan, but she caught the warmth in Mrs Napier's eyes and brightened. 'I'm not used to being waited on,' she commented, and Mrs Napier laughed.

'You could do with some spoiling. You're far too thin, you know.'

Eagerly, Linette tackled the meat pie and vegetables, 'Slim is the correct word, Mrs Napier.'

'Well, whatever it is, Linette,' Brent's mother looked down at herself, 'it certainly doesn't apply to me. In polite circles, I think I might be referred to as "ample".'

Linette shook her head. 'You're just right for your——' She stopped, afraid of having almost offended her listener.

'My age. That's all right, dear. Like your uncle, I'm in my fifties and not afraid to admit it.'

Linette, halfway through the food on her plate, said reminiscently, 'My aunt was like you. Not too fat, not too thin.' She pushed her plate aside, asking shyly, 'Is there any more to come?'

Mrs Napier laughed happily. 'A second course. Chocolate mousse?'

Linette nodded vigorously, accepting the dish. 'I bet my uncle appreciates your cooking. I cook because I have to, not like you. I'm sure you cook because you love it.'

'I certainly do.' Mrs Napier removed her apron and sat at the table watching her mousse disappear.

Her dress was half-sleeved and simply designed, in a fabric which Linette longed to touch to judge its quality. She was certain it was as expensive as it looked.

Linette said spontaneously, 'You—you look so right sitting there.'

Mrs Napier laughed, murmuring, 'Thank you.' She looked around. 'Aileen Napier, queen of the kitchen, in an ancient cottage in the heart of this lovely countryside. Yes, that's always been my ambition.'

'Is that why you wanted to come and live here?'

Mrs Napier nodded without speaking.

'Would you like some coffee?' she asked, taking Linette's empty dish.

Linette looked up with some surprise. 'Why, did my uncle have some?'

'No. He said it didn't agree with him.'

'We don't usually drink anything after lunch.' Linette frowned. Somewhere there was a truth she felt she should hit upon, the key to something, but what it was eluded her detection.

Mrs Napier sat down again, having washed and dried the final dish. 'Do you—like the other cottage, Linette?'

'Very much,' Linette answered, surprised by the woman's uncharacteristic hesitancy.

'Good. That means it won't take you long to get used to it, doesn't it? I mean, if you hated the place, we would have to rethink the whole situation.'

Linette shook her head. 'My uncle agreed to your coming to live here, which means he must like you.' She pushed around her place mat. 'He doesn't take to everybody.' She gave a quick, sideways smile. 'And if he doesn't, he comes out with it, just like that.'

'I know. I judged that that was his way the day I waited for you to serve me, and heard him talking about me!'

Linette laughed. 'One thing I am sure of is that he'll love your cooking!'

Later, when she sat alone at the window of her new home, Linette experienced a sense of gladness. It was the atmosphere of the place which had appealed to her from the start. Now, in the quietness, it wrapped around her and she felt cocooned, safe. A place of her own—something many people the world over longed for—and she had it, was surrounded by it—and was content.

It was a contentment that was not to last. Out of the silence came the sound of an approaching car. It drew up with a squeal of brakes and the hooting of a horn outside the front entrance of Wealden Grange.

A high-pitched voice greeted what must have been a warm welcome, judging by the number of 'darlings' scattered about the response. Brent's girl-friend, Nita

Cutler, had come for the evening.

Jealousy stirred like dust in a breeze, whipping up until it wrapped about Linette like a sandstorm. After Brent's kisses and a passion only barely leashed as he had lain beside her in the night, what else was he now doing but demonstrating how little it had meant to him?

Unable to remain seated and let her imagination make a meal of Brent's girl-friend's visit to his home, Linette walked around the room aimlessly. Her feet took her upstairs and she went from one room to the other, finishing in the second bedroom.

This she had not seen before, having believed it to be empty. To her surprise, it was fully furnished. Even the bed was made up, the floor carpeted and the window adorned with attractive curtains. It was thoughtful of Brent, she mused, to have provided her with a guestroom, although who he had had in mind when giving instructions for it to be fitted with furniture, she could not imagine. Unless it was her parents?

From downstairs there came the sound of a telephone ringing. Racing down, she traced the sound to the main living-room, finding the instrument on a small table across the room. A high-backed chair had hidden it from view.

Putting the receiver to her ear, she took a breath to state the number, only to realise she did not know it. 'Linette Kemp here,' she said.

'At last I've found you!' Leslie's voice exclaimed. 'First I phoned your home, and a woman answered. I was so surprised that it wasn't you, I couldn't get the words out. I think she must have thought I was infantile, or something.'

'That was Mrs Napier. She's living there now.'

'So I gathered, but where's your uncle gone?'

'Nowhere. He just has a new sub-tenant.'

'Which means——'

'Mr Napier got his way. He pitchforked me here as if I were a bundle of hay and here I stay. Did Mrs Napier give you my number?'

'Well, she said she knew you were on the phone——'

'Which was more than I did!'

Leslie laughed. 'But she suggested I phoned her son for your number.'

'You did?' Linette hoped Leslie had not picked up the note of dismay.

There was a chuckle. 'A woman answered there, too.'

'His girl-friend.' Had Leslie noticed the trace of bitterness?

It seemed he was deaf to all undertones and wanted only to get his own message across. 'I didn't like the sound of her. A rather superior type, I imagined. She put me on to Mr Napier who obliged with your number. I thought——' Leslie hesitated, 'well, that he sounded rather abrupt.'

'Perhaps you disturbed something.' The acidity this time was surely obvious.

Apparently it passed Leslie by. He laughed, then pressed on, 'Are you busy, Linette? You know, scrubbing, measuring for chairs and tables and so on?'

'Leslie, you should see the place—like a picture postcard. It's all here, everything provided. You——' Linette smiled at the thought, 'you can come and see the place, if you want.'

It was plain by his eager acceptance that that was what Leslie did want. 'I'll call on the neighbour to look after Jenny, then I'll come straight round.'

While Linette waited for Leslie, she stood at the front window, smiling across the distance that divided her from Wealden Grange. Brent had his visitor, soon she would have hers. Which just about evened things up nicely, she thought, not without a touch of spite.

Putting on the kettle for coffee and setting out two cups and saucers, she heard the sound of crunching feet on the gravel path, and hurrying to the window, she saw that it was Leslie. Flinging open the door, she asked,

'Don't tell me you've walked all the way?'

He looked back over his shoulder. 'I didn't like to drive through the gateway, so I parked my car in the private road.'

'Maybe it's just as well. Mr Napier might drop back in time a few hundred years and decide that his peasant tenant has no right to entertain a male visitor without his consent.'

Leslie smiled at her sarcasm. 'By locking the gates and impounding my car for the night?'

'I wouldn't put anything past him,' Linette muttered darkly, and invited her guest to take a seat.

Leslie gazed round admiringly. 'Your taste?' he enquired.

Linette shook her head. 'Mr Napier's mother's. I suppose you know he really intended the place for my uncle as well as for me?'

'So how did your uncle manage to stay put? Didn't he object to having a strange woman sharing his place with him?'

Linette rubbed her forehead in a bewildered gesture. 'She's so *nice*, Leslie, so understanding. She's got a kind of air about her . . .' Linette shook her head. 'I can't really describe it. My uncle seemed to take to her at once, although he pretended to be grudging about it.'

Leslie nodded and smiled, knowing Linette's uncle. There was a short silence and Linette's mind wandered along the gravel path outside, through the half-circle of trees, and entered the manor house at which earlier she had been staring.

What were they doing over there? Which room were they in? Were they laughing, talking or——? She jerked her thoughts all the way back home. What did it matter to her whether Brent Napier made love to his lady guest? It did, her heart cried, it did!

'Would you like to see over the cottage?' she asked, over-brightly.

Leslie followed her through the door which led to the smaller living-room. 'Useful to have an extra room,' he commented, then followed Linette back into the main room out of which opened the kitchen. He nodded appreciatively. 'Very modern. Nothing seventeenth-century about this,' he indicated the modern equipment, 'and that area has been added on.'

'It would have been so small otherwise,' Linette commented. 'Let's go upstairs.'

The bathroom elicited the same comment as the kitchen, at which Linette laughed. 'The only showers they had in the sixteen-hundreds were the ones provided by the clouds!'

The guest bedroom looked tidy and too unused. Even to Linette, the air in the room was cold, as if it needed human warmth to bring it to life. Having left her own bedroom until last, she switched on the light and led Leslie over to the window.

Since she could see the Grange quite clearly, she guessed it was possible for the cottage to be seen from the Grange. Thus she pulled Leslie to stand beside her with an invitation to look across at Brent Napier's manor house. She dearly hoped that the manor's owner was at that moment looking across at them.

'What does he want,' Leslie wondered, 'with a place that size? Ever been inside it, Lin?'

'Never. Mr Napier told me it's chaotic in there. He's having the whole building renovated.'

'Well, he's got company tonight. I can see a car parked outside the house.'

'It belongs to the woman who answered your call.' Linette did her best to lighten the tone of her voice. 'Her name's Nita Cutler. He told me she works for his company as secretary to one of the top people.' Now she attempted a careless laugh. 'I suspect it's himself, although he said not.'

'Is it the old story, do you think? An affair between boss and secretary?'

Linette's teeth caught at her lower lip to fend off an attack of almost physical pain. 'It looks like it, doesn't it?' she answered at last. She caught at Leslie's arm and even, for a few seconds, let her head droop to his shoulder. Then she disengaged from him and pulled the curtains.

Smiling brightly at Leslie's surprise, she thought vindictively, That should make him think! By 'him' she had not meant Leslie, but he followed her down the wooden stairs with a lighter step. Glancing back over her shoulder, she checked that the light in her bedroom had not been switched off. And that, she told herself, with a pleasing feeling of revenge, should make Brent think yet again.

'Let's make some coffee,' she suggested, going into the kitchen.

Leslie watched her actions, seating himself on a high stool. He seemed preoccupied.

'Is it nice to be waited on?' Linette asked, breaking his reverie.

He looked up sharply, frowning. 'Oh, yes, yes, it is. Life—doesn't get any easier when you're on your own, although Jenny helps me. You know, stops me being completely lonely.'

Linette's heart went out to him, yet she dreaded hearing him repeat his entreaty to her to share his house—although she knew he wanted more than that. As she worked, she felt it was necessary to say something, so she asked,

'Any news of your wife?'

He shook his head and took the tray from Linette's hands. 'Where?' he asked in the living-room. 'On this coffee table?' Linette nodded, bending to pour. Leslie accepted a cup, saying, 'Jane's brought non-communication to a fine art.'

'You'd think she'd at least write to Jenny.'

He sighed, taking a drink and leaning back. 'Jenny invents letters from her mother, then solemnly sits down and "answers" them—you know, scribbles on a piece of paper.'

'I've tried to teach her a few letters. No wonder she's so eager to learn.' Linette felt a lump in her throat. 'To write to an invisible mother!' She drank to disguise her trembling lips. There was another silence, this time initiated by herself.

'Where's the play-group going to meet now, Lin?'

Linette's hand went to her cheek. 'Do you know, Leslie,

I haven't even thought about it. So many things have happened . . .' She frowned. 'Here, I imagine, although I suppose I shall have to ask permission. Brent—Mr Napier——' Had Leslie noticed? He seemed too intent on her answer. 'Mr Napier might object to having small children running around his estate. Not that I'd let them do that, but he'll probably think that's what will happen.'

Leslie finished his coffee, placing his cup and saucer beside Linette's. 'I hope it will continue, Lin,' he said earnestly. 'It gives the neighbour a rest from having Jenny for me and it takes a load off my mind while I'm working.'

'I'll do my best, Leslie. If Mr Napier turns awkward, maybe it can continue at my uncle's cottage, although——' Her puzzlement showed in her eyes.

Why did she feel that even entering the cottage that had so recently been her home was a kind of intrusion? Mrs Napier was just a sub-tenant, nothing more, yet there was something more. If only she could put her finger on that elusive 'something', she fretted.

When Leslie left, the clock in the other room was chiming eleven.

'I'll walk to the gate with you,' Linette offered.

Leslie seemed pleased and helped her on with her jacket. His arm came round her waist as they walked slowly along the narrow road from the cottage. Linette did not mind. It probably made him feel less lonely, she thought.

The visitor's car had gone. Linette assumed that Brent's visitor had insisted on driving when they had gone out to dine or dance or whatever . . . Then she saw a light upstairs in the Grange and guessed that Brent's guest had departed without escort.

At the gate, Leslie thanked her for a happy evening. His hands rested on her shoulders. 'May I?' he asked.

'Kiss me?' Why not? Linette thought. It was an innocent act compared with what Brent and his guest had probably indulged in. The picture which sprang before her eyes in the darkness had her nodding over-eagerly.

The kiss Leslie gave her was not as hesitant as his ques-

tion had been. His arms went round her and by the time
he had finished, Linette knew how much he was missing
his wife's company. In fact, she thought, pushing back her
hair, I'd like to bet it was not Linette Kemp he was kissing
but Jane, his wife.

With a wave, Leslie left her. Tossing her head at the
light shining out from the Grange, Linette walked back to
the cottage. She saw that her bedroom light was shining
brightly, too. I hope, she told herself vindictively, that's
he's thinking what I wanted him to think!

Locking the front door, she cleared away and washed
the dishes before going up to bed.

The clock was chiming ten downstairs. It was Sunday
morning, so Linette was not over-worried by the comparative lateness of the hour. It's such a comfortable bed,
she thought, turning over, it was a pity to leave it. Her
eyelids drooped and she slid into a light sleep.

It had not been light enough to warn her of a series of
events. A key had unlocked her entrance door, firm footsteps had climbed the stairs. Her bedroom door had
creaked open. It had all happened in her dream and it
had brought a man to stand beside the bed.

In fact, it was a re-run of the events of two nights ago,
when Brent Napier had snatched her up and abducted her
. . . Her heart started to thump as awareness returned, and
a moistness appeared on her forehead. A man *had* broken
into her house, a man *was* standing beside her bed.

Her eyes flew open. 'What do you want? How did you
get in? I didn't invite you!'

Brent smiled tauntingly and he held up a duplicate of
her own key. 'You didn't realise I had this, did you? It's a
good thing I checked before I came that your boy-friend's
car had gone and that he hadn't stayed the night.
Otherwise . . .' His narrowed eyes said the rest.

'If he had, you wouldn't have dared to walk in.'

'Wouldn't I?'

She was half sitting up now. 'Because if you had, I

would have repaid the compliment the next time your girl-friend came to visit you.'

The coolness of his regard told her she had displeased him. The knowledge made her smile up at him defiantly.

' "We're just friends", you said, when I challenged you about Leslie Dickins.'

'Well, it's true, we—we are.'

'You can say that, when you walked him so lovingly to the gate, and when he kissed you goodnight so passionately?'

Linette traced the pattern on her quilt cover. 'He wasn't kissing me, he was really kissing his wife.'

'So you're going to marry him?' The question was like a whiplash and she cowered involuntarily from the anger in his eyes.

'No, of course not. I meant that he was kissing his wife in his imagination.'

He made a sneering, dismissive sound. 'Don't give me that sentimental rubbish, Linette. Especially as I saw the light on in this room for most of the evening.'

'I knew you would!' She had intended to speak triumphantly, but the words had a dismayed ring about them.

He returned from the window, through which he had been staring. 'I trust you had an enjoyable evening.' She hated his contempt. 'No wonder you're still in bed.' He strolled to the bedside. 'I've a mind to join you there.'

Linette shrank away. To have him lying beside her in love—this she would have welcomed with all her heart, but in hate—the thought terrified her. Brent Napier making love while feeling nothing but contempt for the woman on the receiving end, especially if she loved him, would be hellish indeed.

Looking up at him, she was sure her uncertainty showed. His shirt was partly unbuttoned, his belted slacks were well-worn and snug-fitting. It seemed he had not yet bothered to shave and there was a black shadow around his cheeks and chin.

'I'm sorry,' she said, pulling up the covers as she sat upright, 'but I'm getting dressed now.'

'Go ahead.' He folded his arms. 'I'm not stopping you.'

'You are, by being here.'

'If you can undress in front of your boy-friend, you can dress in front of me.'

'I object to your assumption that Leslie and I——' She remembered her trick of leaving the light on, thus provoking him to believe that she and Leslie had spent an intimate evening. So I've only myself to blame, she thought, staring miserably at the opposite wall, if Brent now thinks exactly what I planned for him to think.

Her bare shoulders lifted and fell with a sigh. 'I'll just have to stay here all day, then, won't I?'

His fingers went to his shirt buttons, unfastening the remainder. 'It's your choice,' he remarked casually, although his eyes were busy running over her arms and ruffled hair, 'but if you think I intend to let you lie there alone, then think again.'

His shirt was free of his waistband now, and Linette's wondering eyes ran eagerly over his lean waist and athletic build. The desire to touch him was so strong, she closed her eyes. In that moment, he moved swiftly towards her, slipping the straps from her shoulders and tipping her face to take a hard kiss.

He sat sideways and pulled her across him, but she fought him with hands and arms and nails. The nightdress, in the struggle, slipped down, revealing the provocative fullness of her breasts. His head bent to kiss their yielding softness, cupping each one in turn with hard hands.

Her head fell back in her joy at his touch, but it shook negatively and she cried, 'No, no, Brent, I won't let you be my lover!'

His head lifted and his gaze held a flash of steel. 'One at a time is enough, is it, then?' He pushed her from him. 'You're right. After your having spent a passionate evening with Leslie Dickins, I wouldn't touch you for a fortune!'

He looked down at her piquant shape, which still held

the marks his hands and his lips had made. Following his gaze and colouring deeply, Linette hastily drew her night-dress into place.

Her flushed face lifted to his and she saw that he was fastening his shirt and tucking it in. Was this a favourable time to ask a favour of him?' She doubted it, but it was a question that had to be asked that day. 'Brent?'

'Yes?' he answered curtly turning at the door.

'May I ask you something?'

'Is it important?'

'It's—it's business.'

He paused, appeared to hesitate, then snapped, 'Later.' With that she had to be content.

Brent strode from the room, jerking the door into place.

## CHAPTER SEVEN

FOR a while, Linette sat staring towards the window, watching the curtains rise and fall in the breeze. By pulling those across last night and deliberately leaving the light on, she knew she had asked for his censure. I'll just have to take it, she told herself. She sighed. If only she had paused to consider the consequences of her action.

Wearing a short-sleeved pink shirt and midnight blue cords, she went down the stairs, only to stop halfway. Brent was stretched out, long legs crossed at the ankle, in an armchair, reading the Sunday paper! Since she did not take one, Linette knew he must have brought it with him. How long did he intend to stay?

Refusing to ask the question he was probably waiting for, she continued on her way. When she had reached the foot of the stairs, Brent glanced over the top of the newspaper, gave her a quick scan, then returned to reading it.

Doubtfully she gazed at him. Should she offer breakfast? It would mean cooking for two, whereas she usually did not even bother to cook for one.

'I'm going to eat,' she announced, and mentally sat back on her heels to await the reply. When it came, it was succinct.

'Go ahead. I've eaten.'

Passing him on the way to the kitchen, she held herself stiffly, but he did not move a muscle as she passed.

Making toast and boiling an egg, she decided to make enough coffee for two. If she made it for herself alone, he would almost certainly turn awkward and ask for a non-existent cup.

Carrying her meal into the living-room, she lowered it to the table. 'I eat in here on Sundays,' she explained, yet annoyed with herself for doing so.

She waited for the sarcastic comment, but Brent just nodded and turned a page of the colour supplement. With his back to her, she found she could almost succeed in blotting out the sight, if not the thought, of him.

Digging into her egg with enthusiasm, and nibbling pieces of toast, she had become so absorbed she had failed to notice he had changed his place of seating and was watching her with some amusement.

His gaze drew hers and she stopped in mid-bite. She put down her egg spoon and watched, fascinated, his every movement. He dropped the newspaper to the floor and rose, lifting his arms high and stretching luxuriously.

When he had finished, his hands found his hips. 'Haven't you ever seen a man stretching his limbs before?' His sarcastic question jerked her from her frozen position and she coloured faintly, finishing her meal. Brent wandered over to the table and lifted the lid of the coffee pot. 'That's a lot for one person.'

'I included you,' she responded tartly. She indicated two cups.

'Very thoughtful.' He eyed her mockingly. 'You're not usually so eager to please your landlord. This "something" you want to ask me must be important to you.'

'It is,' she sorted the cups, 'but that's not why I made

extra coffee. Milk?' she asked sweetly.

His distrust of her stretched smile and too-bright glance elicited an assessing look from him. He nodded but declined the sugar, carrying his cup and saucer back to the chair. 'Finished eating?' he asked. 'Good. Come and join me.'

Taking the chair he had first occupied, Linette took a sip or two, wishing she could forget what had happened between them that morning. The throb of his touch was still with her and this, combined with the sight of his lean, lazy figure caused a drumbeat of primitive desire to hammer at her pulses.

As he drank he watched her and she fought to smother her embarrassment under a cloak of simulated unconcern. 'I'm listening,' he said, breaking the silence.

'Well,' Linette began, then took too-large a swallow and choked a little, growing annoyed with herself for revealing to him how nervous she was. Recovering, she put her cup aside. 'It's about the play-group.'

Eyes hooded as his head went back against the chair, he commented, 'I guessed that was coming.' He finished his coffee, putting his cup next to hers. 'Carry on.'

'Would you mind if——' No, that was too timid. 'Is there any objection to——' Come out with it, her uncle would have said. 'I would like,' she declared, her voice firm at last, 'to have the children here, in my—this—cottage. Please,' she finished jerkily.

'And have them running free and unrestrained all over the estate?'

'I *knew* you'd say that! I told Leslie——' Oh no, she thought, dismayed. That name was surely the key word to ensuring the eruption of his anger.

His anger did not erupt, it slithered, snake-like, from his tightened lips. 'Ah, now I know.' He was out of his chair and towering over her. 'The play-group must go on for the sake of the man in your life.'

'He's not——' she started to say, but knew it would be futile to make the denial. She had left the bedroom light on, she had baited the trap. Brent had swallowed the bait whole, but the trap had snapped shut—on her!

'It's not just Leslie,' she asserted, avoiding his eyes, 'all the mothers benefit, too.'

He would not halt the attack now. His interest had fixed on Jenny's father to the exclusion of all the other children's mothers. He bent to grasp her wrists, hauling her up to face him. 'Admit you broke up that marriage, and that you're now in the middle of an affair with the husband.'

Linette twisted her wrists but could not free them. Her head lifted high. 'I'll admit nothing. I deny both accusations.'

'Deny them as much as you like. I saw you both at your bedroom window. I saw you draw the curtains. I saw the loving way he held you as you walked to the gate, and I saw the passionate goodnight kiss. Put them all together, shake them up and you get a potent cocktail.'

'And,' she flung back, fire in her eyes, 'I saw your lady-love arrive. I heard her "darling" you. What an enjoyable evening *you* must have had! Anyway, why should you care whether or not I'm sleeping with a man? You and I aren't engaged. We mean nothing to each other.'

It was, she knew in her heart, a blatant lie. Brent Napier had grown to mean everything to her, yet they could never meet without quarrelling, without giving pain for pain.

He threw her wrists from him and she rubbed them ruefully. If he saw her trembling lip, she didn't care. It was all going so wrong for her, and this man was the cause, the wrecker of her contentment, of her happy way of life.

Sinking back into the chair, she said despondently, 'If the play-group can't be held here, it will have to be cancelled. I can't have it at my uncle's cottage now. I don't want the kiddies getting under your mother's feet—although my guess is that your mother would love them.'

There was a long pause, yet she did not look at him to gauge his reactions. 'Your mother,' she went on, uncaring now if she hurt his feelings, 'is one of the kindest, most thoughtful women I know. She's wonderful. In fact, I simply don't know how she could have had a son like you!'

Still that lower lip trembled and, to her dismay, it sounded as though the damned-up tears had invaded her voice. Brent still had not spoken. Curiosity lifted her head. Why had he not retaliated against her goading words?

He looked down at her unhappy face. His own face showed no signs of emotion. It simply wasn't fair, she thought, that he could so successfully hide his feelings. He walked to the glass doors which gave on to the back lawn and flower beds. Pausing for a few seconds, he walked back.

'You can have your play-group here. Just make sure the children are kept under control.'

Linette was about to reply indignantly that she always did, when caution closed her lips. The point had been won, although whether or not he had ever intended to refuse, she would never know.

'Thank you,' she whispered, seeking his eyes.

Brent's finger feathered the shadowed area beneath her eyes. It came away wet. Now both her lips were trembling. Had she softened his heart? It seemed that nothing would do that. He gave a brief nod and left her.

It was a sultry afternoon. The clouds hung low, the breeze was slight. Linette knew she would find her uncle in his garden. Today, he was tending the vegetables at the rear of his cottage.

'Uncle Godfrey!' she greeted him happily. She touched his shoulder and he straightened from his digging. 'It's as if I've been away months.'

He smiled his slow smile. 'How are you getting on, Lin?'

'Fine, Uncle, now I've settled in. You?' She glanced at the cottage. 'And Mrs Napier?'

'Fine, like you.' He bent to his work. 'I call her Aileen now—that's her name. She suggested it.'

'That's—that's wonderful. How do you spend your evenings? Round at the George and Dragon?'

'I don't go so often. When I do, Aileen comes with me.

She enjoys a chat with my friends. They've started bringing their wives.'

Linette's eyes crinkled. 'Trust Mrs Napier to discover a way of saving marriages from being broken up by the Demon Drink! So she chats with the wives?'

Godfrey nodded. 'When we don't go there, we watch television or listen to some records.'

'But Uncle, you haven't got a record player.'

'Aileen's brought her hers from the big house. She's round there now, collecting some more of her things. The builders want to start on the two rooms she uses.'

Linette nodded, then frowned. This was a side of her uncle she had never guessed was there. He had had a happy married life with her aunt Amy, but she had been a homely person. Mrs Napier was homely too, she reflected, but in a different way. She was brisk and bright, giving the impression of never failing to rise to a challenge. Aunt Amy had possessed a comfortable, contented personality, wanting no more of life than she actually had—a good, hardworking husband who was blunt but entirely honest.

It seemed to Linette's bewildered mind that Mrs Napier and her Uncle Godfrey made a strange pair. If her uncle had not wanted the woman to share his home, he would have said so outright, stubbornly refusing to allow her entry. It could only mean one thing, Linette concluded.

By allowing her, Linette, to be forcibly removed by the landlord, he had demonstrated his preference for the company of someone in his own age group. I can't blame him, Linette decided. If things had been the other way round, wouldn't I have preferred to share a place with someone nearer to my age?

'Uncle?' Linette began. He nodded to indicate that he was listening. 'Brent—Mr Napier has given permission for me to hold the play-group at my—his cottage. So you won't be troubled by the children three times a week.'

'They weren't any trouble,' he said gruffly.

'I know that, but there's more space there for them to run around.'

Godfrey nodded again, and Linette made her way home. The main entrance gates, she noticed, were wide open. As she walked through them, a large car approached. At the sight of it, her heart began to thud. Coming from that direction, only one person could possibly be driving it— then she saw her guess was wrong.

The driver was a woman. She was smiling and her hand lifted in a cheerful wave. Mrs Napier braked and pushed her head out. 'Linette, how are you, my dear? Does the new cottage agree with you?'

Linette smiled. 'Now I've settled in, it's fine, thanks.'

'Well, if there's anything you need, just ask my son.' She gestured to the rear seat. 'I've been pushed out of my rooms. I've got the rest of my belongings with me.'

Linette nodded. 'My uncle told me. I've just been to see him.'

'He's very long-suffering to put up with me, plus all my bits and pieces.'

'Well,' Linette shook her head in bewilderment, 'once he would have objected, but now,' she smiled, 'you seem to have mellowed him.'

Mrs Napier laughed and her round, still youthful face lit up. 'I doubt it. The passage of time usually does the mellowing.' She frowned playfully. 'Now I wonder if he still thinks of me as a "fussy old bag".'

Linette recalled her uncle's disparaging remark about his landlord's mother the day she had lined up with others to be served at the fruit and vegetable stall. 'I'm quite certain he doesn't,' Linette answered, smiling. 'He wouldn't spend his evenings with you if he did.'

Mrs Napier's hand came through the window and patted Linette's shoulder. 'Thanks for that, dear.' She prepared to drive on. 'I imagine it's my cooking that's found its way to his heart, not me!'

Watching the car being driven away, Linette wondered how many cars Brent possessed. It bore his unmistakable stamp. It was large, sleek and expensive.

'Time on your hands?' The question came from behind

her, from the direction of the Grange, and its owner, whose approach must have been hidden by the sound of the car, stood regarding her. His thumbs were hooked over the belt of his slacks, his attitude easy yet curiously alert. The glance from his brown eyes slipped over her and Linette wished she had worn something better than the jeans and blouse she had put on that morning. Clothes, she thought, to bring a look of admiration to his eyes, instead of the touch of mockery with which he seemed always to regard her.

'I've been visiting my uncle, telling him about the play-group.' With her head on one side, she looked up at him. 'Tomorrow morning, do you object if the main gates are left open so that the children's parents can deposit them here?'

He indicated that they should walk towards her cottage. It was so good having him beside her that she felt oddly complete, as if she were his and he hers and their future paths met and merged, never to part.

'Does this mean that you'll want them open three times a week?'

Her heart sank. Was he going to be difficult? 'It does. Do you want to call the whole thing off?'

They were at the cottage door, facing each other. 'You're prepared to give in to my wishes that easily? After the fight you put up when I nearly had you and your uncle evicted?'

His smile challenged and she hit back, 'That was different. This is your property,' she indicated the manor house, the grounds of the estate, 'and I'd hate you to bring a charge of trespassing against the children and their mothers.'

His eyes twinkled mischievously and his fist brushed her chin. 'Cheeky madam! After that, I've a mind to refuse.'

Linette's shoulders lifted and fell.

Brent turned her and pointed to the door. 'Your key or mine?' His hand pushed into his pocket was quicker than hers. He opened the door and they entered.

He went on, 'I don't see the logic of your argument. True, this is all owned by me, but so is the other cottage.'

She grinned. 'Okay, you win.'

He laughed. 'I can see why your boy-friend is so taken with you.'

'Boy-friend?' Her frown was genuine. 'You don't mean Leslie? At that moment, he couldn't have been farther from my mind.'

'You made love with him all evening, and you've forgotten him by the next day? Some girl-friend you are!'

She smiled up at him. 'But that's the point. I'm not his girl-friend.'

Momentarily his jaw hardened, then it softened back into a smile. 'Come for a drive?'

'I wouldn't say no.'

Brent picked up a handful of curls and tugged them, plainly provoked by her impish grin. 'Come on, then.'

They drove to Bourton-on-the-Water, and walked among the crowds of tourists. Souvenir shops had opened their doors and people gazed in the windows, hunted for postcards and wandered about inside, looking for gifts. In the gardens of the Old New Inn was the famous Model Village which reproduced in minute detail the village itself. The golden stone of the real-life houses shone in the afternoon sunshine as Brent led Linette across one of the many small bridges spanning the River Windrush, a tributary of the River Thames. Couples passed them hand-in-hand. Brent looked at them, then at Linette, and took her hand.

Smiling, unable to hide her happiness, she let him entwine his fingers with hers. This was not the first time she had visited the town, but on no other occasion had she been filled with such intense pleasure. They stood by the riverside and watched their reflections. Willows wept into the clear water, yellow flowers caught and admired their own images. Turning back and gazing along the faintly rippling water, they could see the other low, arched stone bridges making the crossing of the water easy for tourists and villagers alike.

After a tea of scones and jam and cream, followed by a choice of cakes, they made their way back to the car. Brent operated the electrically controlled windows and there was a rush of sweet, fresh air into the interior.

Brent inhaled. 'The freshness calls me to the high places all around us. We'll go and find the open spaces.'

They made their way in a north-westerly direction, parking the car just off the road. They walked, hand-in-hand, on to the private land which took them to the Rollright Stones, a circle of standing stones dating, Brent told her, from the Bronze Age.

'Which makes them,' he added, 'around three thousand, five hundred years old. These are known as the King's Men, and over there, across the road, is the King's Stone.'

Warm though she was, Linette shivered. A strong breeze blew, but she knew that the feeling of chill was caused also by the response within her to the atmosphere of the place, the wonder inside her at the stones' great age.

The children from a visiting family obviously felt no such respect for history. Linette watched them clamber over the pieces of rock which were gouged and eroded by time and the elements.

Brent, having felt her shiver, put his arm around her shoulders. It was as though he had guessed the cause, since he did not question her. Maybe he had felt a similar response? That, she told herself, she could hardly believe. He might be holding her in a gesture of comfort, but she must never forget that inside, he was as hard and forbidding as the Rollright Stones themselves.

It would take as many thousands of years to wear his true personality down as it had taken to make a mark on these objects, and yet still they endured. What hope, then, she thought, for a change in Brent's unyielding character?

Having gained the 'open spaces' to which Brent had referred, Linette stood on the grassland and gazed with wonder at the view. The hills stretched one behind the other into the very distance. The keen wind was up here, too. It lifted her hair, tossed her curls and made her hug herself. Brent stood beside her, staring, too, lost in that great distance. It was distancing him from her.

Linette seized his arm, shaking it. 'Isn't it magnificent, Brent?' she asked, endeavouring to bring him back to her. His head came round and she discovered she had succeeded more effectively than she realised. His mouth was curved, and there was only the smallest amount of irony there.

'So are you,' he pulled slightly away the better to survey her, 'with your ins and outs and tantalising curves. One day,' he teased, 'I should love to draw a relief map of your contours. Come on, we'll find somewhere to sit.' Across the road was a wooden gate fixed in a dry-stone wall. 'I know the owner of this farm. He won't object if we make use of a small patch for a rest.'

The gate was securely fastened, but Brent ignored the fact, swinging himself over and holding out a hand as Linette followed his example. She jumped to the ground and Brent caught and held her. Her face was uplifted to him, but if she had expected his kiss, she did not receive one.

He grinned as if knowing what was in her mind and put her from him. Linette knew her face fell, but turned it to the view, hoping he had not noticed. There was a bleat of sheep farther down the hill. They were chewing contentedly and ignored the interlopers.

'Looks as though they don't object to sharing their pasture,' Brent commented. 'Here, near this tree.' He went on to his haunches, waiting for her to join him. When she hesitated, he reached up to her waist and pulled her down. They tumbled on to the grass and Linette found herself entangled with him. His long legs were mixed with hers, while one of his arms was around her waist and his free hand at the back of her head.

He rolled on to his back, hauling her on top of him. 'Now you've got me where you want me,' he quipped.

'Who said I want you?' she asked with an impudent smile.

He rolled her over until their positions were reversed. 'I

could make you, sweetheart—oh yes, I could make you.'

Linette closed her eyes on the light in his eyes. Almost immediately, she opened them, returning his smile. With the back of her hand, she rubbed over his cheeks which, even at that comparatively early hour, felt roughened. His chest hair pushed through the thin material of his open-necked shirt. In the toss and tumble of their bodies, Linette's blouse buttons had been tugged apart and the bristly sensation made her skin prickle.

'Is this,' she whispered, wishing his long-awaited kiss would materialise, 'what they call a roll in the long grass?'

Brent pressed the tip of her nose. 'I wouldn't know.' His eyes dwelt upon her naturally pouting lips. 'My female companions usually face me across a dinner table, while soft-footed waiters buzz around us eager to please. I've never had a girl-friend who would dream of untidying herself by lying in a field with gnats buzzing round, eager only to please themselves. And,' he levered himself on to an elbow while Linette experienced a stab of disappointment as the pressure of him left her, 'instead of the bleat of sheep, there's usually taped music.'

'Give me chewing sheep any time,' Linette declared. 'They're much more real than chewing diners.'

He turned back to her, pulling her on to her side. 'A real country girl, aren't you?'

'Through and through. Ever since I came to live here, in fact, eighteen months ago. And that's the difference between us,' she went on, touching his chin, 'you're a city man from top to toe. We could never meet on the same plane.'

There was a dangerous glint in his eye. 'Let me demonstrate to you that there's one plane on which we can most definitely meet.'

The kiss he had been withholding came at last. Linette went to him unresistingly as his arms slid under her and hers curled of their own accord around his neck. His mouth made unhesitatingly for the target, parting her lips and forcing an entry. Her wordless sounds of eager response seemed to urge him on.

His hand slid between them, jerking at her blouse until it was free, and that same hand insinuated itself into the gap, gliding over her midriff and finding the soft curves of her breasts.

Her fingers raked through his hair, then with frantic movements stroked it down. They were as possessed as her body by his kisses and caresses. A rising need for fulfilment took hold, and she never wanted him to stop his plunder of her senses.

Stop he did, however, lifting his head at last, but without relinquishing his ungentle hold on her breasts. 'You're magnificent,' he said softly, 'all fire and desire and demand. A man couldn't ask for more.'

At last he removed his possessive hand, only to rest it gently round her throat. 'You're fresh air and sun-drowned uplands, wild flowers and,' he buried his face in the inner curve of her shoulder, 'full of country scents. And,' he raised his head, 'I've proved my point. There is a plane we can meet on. In no way can you deny that, not after the way you've just responded to me.'

Linette breathed deeply, about to shake her head, then it changed to a nod. 'Perhaps you're right. But, as I said once before, we were——' she was about to tell a lie as far as her own feelings were concerned, 'only doing, as the saying goes, what comes naturally.' She tried a grin for size, but her heart wasn't in it. 'I'm quite sure with you it came very naturally indeed. You've had so much practice.'

Brent jerked her to her side and a sharp slap cracked on the breeze. 'That should put you in your place!'

'Landlord and tenant again, Mr Napier?' she shot at him, rubbing her stinging flesh.

'No, man and woman.' His tone was short. He stood up and caught her hand pulling her to her feet. 'We're homeward bound. Otherwise, heaven knows what I'll do to you.'

Home, he'd said, Linette thought as they made for the farm gate. He had a home. It belonged to him. In a way, she had a home. The only snag was that it, too, belonged to him. One thing must never happen, she vowed. Never would *she* belong to him.

Hadn't he as good as told her just now that she was simply not his type? What would he do with 'fresh air and wild flowers' sitting across the table from him? He needn't worry, she thought with a touch of after-bliss bitterness, I won't make any demands on him, not now or ever.

He was over the gate and waiting, arms spread. She jumped down, trying to evade them, but they went round her, holding her to him until she had to appeal for release in order to breathe.

He laughed, caught her hand and led her back to the car. It was a silent drive at first, then as they left the uplands behind and drove through historic villages, the front gardens packed with flowers, Linette's thoughts began to surface into questions.

'Why did your mother decide against living in the manor cottage, Brent? Why did it have to be my uncle's place?'

The broad shoulders lifted and fell beneath the half-opened shirt. 'Said she didn't want to live in her son's shadow, that it would look as if she was keeping watch on my comings and goings and prying into my life. They were her sentiments, not mine.'

The answers seemed reasonable enough, but Linette still felt puzzled. 'How long do you think she'll stay in my uncle's cottage?'

'Indefinitely.'

A hand seemed to squeeze her heart. 'What about my uncle? Has he got to share it with her for the rest of his life? Or,' the bitterness was creeping back, 'have you got secret plans for him, just as you had for me?'

A quick, speaking glance came her way, but he drove on in silence. The gates were open and another car was parked in the drive. 'Your mother's here?' Linette asked quickly.

'She is. How did you know?' His voice was detached, he

was back to his 'city man' image.

'The car—I saw her in it earlier this afternoon. It's a big one. It's one of yours, isn't it? I expect she's finished moving her things.'

He got out and Linette followed. 'I asked her to tea,' he said.

The words, 'Yes, please,' were on her tongue when she realised the invitation to join them had not come. Her head lifted high in the face of the silent put-down. *You have no place in this family*, he was saying.

'Thank you for a pleasant afternoon,' she said, and turned to go.

His hand caught her wrist. 'Is that all it was? Pleasant?'

She frowned, pretending incomprehension. 'Why, should I have said unpleasant?'

He threw her hand from him and locked the car. A wave came from one of the many windows in the Grange. Linette guessed whose hand it was and, with a genuine smile, waved back. It was an effort to ease away the droop of her shoulders, but she managed it all the way back to her cottage door.


'Uncle Godfrey,' Linette called to the busy figure already at work in the flower garden, 'I've come to direct the mothers to the Grange gates.'

Godfrey lifted a hand in acknowledgement and carried on with his work.

The mothers heard the news of the change of venue with surprise. 'You mean Mr Napier doesn't mind? He won't charge us with trespassing, will he, if we drive them on to his estate?'

Each one seemed to be serious in her questioning, which made Linette reflect on the image of Brent Napier which people seemed to hold—as a man not only to be reckoned with but even feared.

She smiled with as much reassurance as she could muster, in view of her own frequent confrontations with him. 'There is a human side to him,' she asserted, and did

not pause to consider that they might wonder how she
knew.

They smiled their relief and promised they would wait
with the children until she arrived. Leslie was, as usual,
the last to appear and she asked him for a lift. Jenny
moved up happily, making room and grabbed Linette's
hand as they drove along the private road, entering the
grounds through the gates.

'As you can see,' Leslie commented, slowing down to
brake, 'somebody is still missing her maternal parent.'

Linette looked down at the 'somebody', who smiled up
at her. 'I don't think,' the little girl said, 'my mummy will
ever come back now, Linette.'

Leslie gave Linette a dismayed look, saying silently, She
understood what I said. Linette ruffled Jenny's hair. 'Never
mind, poppet, you love your daddy, don't you? He looks
after you and reads to you and puts you to bed, doesn't
he?'

There was a nod, then small hands pushed at Linette.
'Get out, get out,' the little girl sang. 'I want to go to my
friends.' Jenny clambered over Linette's lap, and was
lifted to the ground.

Leslie's hand rested on Linette's arm. 'I'll be alone this
evening, like all the other evenings. If you're not busy . . .'

Linette thought, He certainly knows how to touch my
sympathy. Aloud, she answered, 'I'll call you some time
today. Okay?'

Leslie smiled and preceded the other cars back to the
main road.

Most of the morning was spent in showing the children
'her little home', as Linette called it. She considered it
necessary, in order to help them to become acclimatised to
their different surroundings. The old toys, however, were
greeted with joy, and the three hours passed quickly.

After her midday meal, Linette dressed in her oldest
clothes and returned to her uncle's cottage. She had always
enjoyed her sessions of digging or planting or thinning out
the vegetables, while maybe her uncle worked in the flower

garden or among the fruit bushes.

Pushing open his gate, she saw that he was in fact among the flowers. Standing beside him, she watched his movements for a while. He had grunted at her appearance, but as she had anticipated, said nothing. He did speak, at last.

'What do you want, Lin?' His question surprised her.

'To help you, as I always do, Uncle.'

There came a noise of vigorous digging from around the back of the cottage, and out of Linette's sight. 'Who's acting my part of gardener's mate?' she asked with a touch of mischief. Then a thought rocked the boat of her playfulness, upsetting it completely. 'Not—not Mrs Napier?'

'Aileen, that's right,' Godfrey answered, nodding. 'Keen gardener she is, just as she told me.'

'So you don't need my help any more, Uncle.' Linette made it a statement on a note of unbelieving laughter.

'That's right, lass. I've got all I need in the way of help now.'

A declaration which was, in its way, as unemotional and dismissing as any Brent Napier might have made.

'You don't mean it, Uncle Godfrey?'

His head bobbed towards the rear gardens. 'See for yourself, lass. She's doing well, is Aileen. Got herself some strong boots, gloves, plus some old clothes. If I'm not careful, she'll be catching up with me and asking for more before I've finished my bit here.'

Mrs Napier appeared. 'I thought I heard your voice,' she said, smiling cheerfully at Linette. 'I didn't think Godfrey was the sort to talk to himself!'

First names, so friendly . . . yet the difference between them, Linette thought, dumbfounded. Mrs Napier with her aura of chatty coffee mornings, arranger of fêtes and bazaars, gossip over afternoon teas. Uncle Godfrey with his monosyllabic turn of phrase, his bluntness and no-nonsense attitude to life. How did they manage to live in such harmony? Mrs Napier, Linette thought, must be a very understanding person indeed. Smiling at her now, Linette realised how much Mrs Napier's good nature must assist her in smoothing away the wrinkles of difference between herself and the man into whose cottage she had moved.

Mrs Napier peeled off her gloves and brushed at her mud-stained jacket. 'Come in, dear, and I'll make us all a cup of tea.'

Knowing how much her uncle disliked being interrupted, except at certain specified times, Linette declined with a smile. Was it also, a small voice asked, the tiniest trace of resentment which lingered as a result of being ousted from what she still regarded as her domain—the kitchen and the garden of her uncle's cottage?

There was one matter which required to be straightened out. 'Tomorrow morning,' Linette said in a voice full of confidence, 'I'll be down as usual, Uncle,' she addressed his bent back, 'to arrange the stall and serve the customers.'

'Linette dear,' Mrs Napier's hand was on her arm, 'there's no need for you to worry yourself with that any longer. Godfrey has agreed that I should take that over. Honestly, dear,' as Linette started to protest, 'I'll enjoy doing it.'

The protestation, Linette thought forlornly, would certainly not have been made through a fear on her part of giving extra work to Mrs Napier.

'Uncle?' she ventured, willing him to tell her that if she liked, she could still act the sales assistant as she had ever since she had resigned from her job in London and joined him in his cottage.

He straightened slowly. 'Aileen suggested it, Lin, and I agreed. There must be plenty for you to do up there,' his head moved in the direction of the Grange, 'like starting a vegetable patch of your own.'

Linette forced a smile. 'What a good idea, Uncle!' Turning to the smiling woman, she declared, 'I don't mind at all. It's a sensible arrangement, isn't it? Well, I'll be getting home——' she backed away, 'there's the cleaning to do,' she had reached the gate, 'and the dusting.' Her hand lifted in a confident wave. ' 'Bye, Uncle, Mrs Napier.'

Until she was out of their sight, Linette walked fast, then slowed to a dragging pace. Evicted, abducted, living in some else's cottage, rent-free and therefore under a permanent obligation to its owner . . . jobless now, and lonely, so lonely it hurt. Whose fault, she asked herself furiously, whose but Brent Napier's?

With a vigour fuelled by pent-up anger, she scrubbed and cleaned and polished. When she had finished, she came to a halt like a misfiring rocket hitting the earth.

Her energy had gone and with it, her anger. Against whom had it been directed, anyway? Brent, his mother, her uncle, herself? The whole set of unbelievable circumstances which had led to this miserable moment?

Getting herself a fruit drink, she went through the glass doors and into what passed as a garden. Sitting on the grass which she supposed she would one day have to coax into a state fit to be called a lawn, she took small swallows, finding the fruity tang strong on her tongue.

It was a few minutes before she realised that the drink was mixed with salt tears. She put the glass down, threw herself full-length, hiding her face in her arms, and gave way to the mix-up of confusion and frustration and apprehension inside her.


## CHAPTER EIGHT


THE tears did not last, but Linette continued to lie there, exhausted from the outburst. Her brain did its best to work on the puzzle of her future. Eventually she would have to move, go eastwards to the London area, find work of some kind. Would her former employer take her back? She decided she could at least make enquiries.

When two hands fastened under her arms, lifting her to her feet, turning her and pulling her against a hard, familiar chest, she went willingly like an animal to shelter in a blizzard.

The shelter this time was two strong arms. Momentarily, they held her away and she fretted to get back to their warmth and protection. 'Linette?'

When he spoke with that kind of tenderness, her legs grew weak. His eyes, filled with an unfamiliar compassion, searched her face. 'What's gone wrong?'

The tone did not reflect his expression. Linette's shoulders lifted. 'Nothing.' The reply, she knew, would not satisfy him. 'Fate. Nothing you—or I—can do anything about.'

Amber eyes narrowed as speculation entered his mind. 'Let me guess. Dickins' wife's gone back to him. End of your affair.'

She pushed away from the security of him, thus casting herself off into a whipped-up sea. 'Wrong! Guess again. No, don't bother. You wouldn't believe it if I told you, since you've got a one-track mind where I'm concerned.'

'You bet I have!' His eyes dropped to appreciate the shape of her, then a hand followed the path his gaze had pioneered. It found the summit of its journey at last, cupping the soft fullness of her with a possessiveness she both rejected yet rejoiced in. 'But at this moment,' his mouth curved in a smile, 'you touch my heart, with your blotchy cheeks and swollen red eyes.'

She pulled away, hating his sarcasm. He followed her through the back door and into the kitchen. 'If I'd known my landlord was coming,' she said, trying to match his mockery, 'I'd have changed into my best clothes.'

'I could put up your rent for that impudence,' he countered, 'if you paid any rent.'

'All right,' she fought back, 'name your price. I promise to pay.'

Brent's eyes dropped to where, a few moments earlier, his hand had lingered. 'You might regret that promise when you hear my "price".'

'You do love hitting a man when he's down, don't you?'

'Man?' He caught her wrists and pulled her arms wide.
'*Man?* With that shape?'

'Oh, you're impossible!' she exclaimed, and he laughed.
Making her way to the living-room, Linette stopped at the
sight of his executive case beside an armchair. As she
turned, she saw he was removing his jacket. 'Why are you
here, anyway?'

'To ask you if you'll feed me this evening. Mary pushed
a note through my door apologising for being unable to do
the usual. One of her kids has got measles.'

'So she'll be off work for quite a while. Do you want me
to feed you *every* evening?'

'After a couple of days, it won't arise for a while. I'm
attending a couple of conferences, one in Holland and
another in Frankfurt.'

That sinking feeling which was overtaking her was
hunger, or even maybe a return of the dismay at her uncle's
rejection of her help. It was nothing whatsoever, she told
herself firmly, to do with the piece of news she had just
been given.

All the same, the question broke free from her stiff lips.
'Going away? For how long?' Did she have to sound so
devastated?

'Impossible to tell. Don't look so upset. You'll be able to
give more time to your boy-friend and his offspring, won't
you, without my being here to spy on his comings and
goings.'

'For that,' her hands went to her hips, 'you can *fish* for
your meal!'

Holding her furious eyes, Brent rolled up each sleeve,
slowly, precisely. Then he swooped, pulling her to him by
her waist, leaving her hanging back and bending over her.
His kiss allowed no sound of protest to escape.

It plundered and it bruised, it forced her to clutch at his
arms, while the ripple of muscle beneath her clawing
fingers increased her excitement as the strength of them
began to squeeze the breath from her lungs.

When he had finished with her, she was encircling his

waist with her arms and resting a burning cheek against his chest. The thudding she heard beneath his ribs drummed out the message that he was not unmoved by their encounter. Sadly she accepted that his strongly-beating heart did not tell her a love story, only one of male physiology reacting to holding a girl in his arms.

'Well,' he said softly, lifting her chin to look into her eyes, 'do I still have to take rod and tackle and catch my meal from the Windrush or the Coln or the Thames, whichever river is the nearest to contain fish?'

Linette shook her head and laughed, and he bent to kiss each eye. Her pulse rate raced and skidded at the action and she wanted him to go on and on kissing her . . .

'It won't be much at such short notice,' she warned, opening the deep-freeze door. 'It's pizza or beefburgers or egg and tomato flan.'

'I'll settle for the flan.'

She looked down at herself. 'I must find some more presentable clothes.' Racing up the stairs, she washed, changed into a blue and white printed dress which fastened with a bow at the neck, combed her hair and hurried down again.

There was a sardonic glint in Brent's eye as he looked her over, but she had no time to make a verbal comeback.

While she darted in and out, setting two places at the table, then hurrying to attend to the food, peeling fruit for the fresh fruit salad whenever she had a spare moment, Brent stretched his legs in a chair and read papers taken from his case.

Now and then he looked up and grinned. When his eyes had mocked her for the fourth time, she stopped in front of him and declared,

'I'm sorry I'm not the poised, cool hostess type you're probably accustomed to when your women cater for you, but since you invited yourself for a meal, you'll just have to accept me as I am.'

The paper he was reading was lowered to his lap. The smile he produced was cynical. 'My *women* don't cater for

me, sweetheart. I take them out to dine. You have to get
your jargon right when your landlord honours you with
his presence at your table.'

'If I—if I had something to throw at you——'

'Throw yourself instead. I'm ready for the consequences
if you are.'

She would not let him have the last word! 'Not on an
empty stomach,' she tossed back, and made for the haven
of the kitchen.

After the meal, Linette prepared herself for his departure. It would be a lonely evening without him, she
thought, and all the lonelier for having had his company
now. To her surprise, he sat on the couch and patted the
empty cushion beside him. 'Come, join me,' he invited. 'I
won't put my arm round you unless you want me to.'

Linette complied, looking at him warily, wishing he
would touch her yet afraid that he might.

'She wants me to,' he said, eyes laughing, and hauled
her across the great divide which separated them. He half
turned her and encompassed her, then nuzzled her neck,
making her skin tingle and forcing a small squeal from
her throat.

His laughter held a sensual pleasure at her response. His
mouth, pressurising hers, pushed her head back to dent
the cushion. Her arms dropped from his shoulders and his
mouth released hers. When she felt his lips skim the sens-
itised skin of her breasts, she gasped, realising how his kiss
must have made her oblivious to the movement of his
fingers unfastening the buttons of her dress.

'Brent, Brent, no, please . . .'

'Yes, sweetheart, yes,' he echoed her own breathless
tone, even in his lovemaking mocking her.

'What's the use? There's no love between us. Is there, is
there?'

'No love,' he echoed again, his mouth leaving her
thrusting softness to the maddening arousal of his hands.
'Nothing between us.' With significance, he added,
'Nothing stands between us—except propriety. And your

ethics, morals, call them what you will, not mine.'

'Ethics?' She was angered into pushing at him.
Surprisingly, he went, rolling back lazily, eyeing her half-
undressed state with faintly insolent eyes.

Re-fastening the buttons with shaking fingers, she
prodded, 'What do you know of ethics? You tried your
eviction tactics, ordered the bailiffs to my uncle's doorstep—and even over the threshold!'

'Yes,' his hooded eyes still lingered on her, as if savouring
still the taste of her softness, 'I'm ruthless, aren't I? I
abducted you from your bed and threw you mercilessly on
to the street. I've made you my target and now I'm hunting
you as relentlessly as a fox after a rabbit. Is that what
you're trying to say?'

Linette regarded him silently, her blue eyes dubious, a
little fearful as his questioning made her wonder which
way he would pounce next. He had thrown her, not on to
the street, but into an even more comfortable bed.

'Well, my little victim, I've certainly got your scent.' He
moved quickly before she could take evasive action and
tugged her round again. He ruffled her hair and buried his
face in its curls. He placed teasing kisses round the back of
her neck. At the cleft between her breasts, he inhaled and
she knew if he forced an opening there again, she would be
lost.

The shrill of the telephone made her jerk away. Before
she could move, he was up and answering. 'Am I Linette?'
His grin was wide. 'No, Mother, you have my assurance
that I'm not. Yes, she's here. Why?'

He listened for a while, his eyes fixed on the dishevelled
girl who sat with her hands clasped.

'When, this afternoon?' he queried. 'Ah, now I understand. Yes, she was in something of a distressed state. Don't
worry, I'll pacify her.' He turned his back on Linette.
'Yes, Mother, I'm aware of what I'm doing. No, I won't
break her heart. You should know, as I do, that it isn't
mine to break. Yes, she's right here. I'll tell her you
called.'

He removed his loosened tie and walked towards her, hands in pockets. 'So that was what the "sulky child" act you staged this afternoon was all about.'

On her feet, Linette confronted him. 'It wasn't an act and I was not sulking! Would you be delighted if you found someone had taken over your job—two jobs really, helping my uncle grow his produce, and selling that produce?'

'You enjoyed doing those things so much it made you distraught to hear that my mother had usurped your place?'

Linette sank back on to the couch. 'I did enjoy them, and it did upset me, but it was something else, too.' She shrugged. 'I can't pinpoint it, but it's got nothing to do with your mother. Just—just a difficulty on my part to accept so many changes in such a short period of time. Yet Uncle Godfrey—he's where he always has been. Of course, I'm pleased about that and that he and your mother get on so well, but . . .'

Her eyes sought his, but although they were fixed on her, they told her nothing of his thoughts.

'I've been pushed around just lately.' Another pause, then an accusing glare. 'And you're the one who's responsible for it all.'

'So, in your eyes, I can't do right.' He seized her arms. 'There's one thing I do right, isn't there?' he said, his eyes hard. 'And that's this.'

Again his lips hit hers. They were hard, bruising, punitive, but she made no sound of protest. She would not give him that satisfaction. The phone rang again and he pushed her away, cursing.

'Now what does my mother want?' he grated. 'Yes?' he demanded of the mouthpiece. 'Who?' His gaze swung to Linette and he watched with satisfaction for a few seconds as she pressed at her burning lips. The receiver was handed over. Linette guessed who was calling and covered the mouthpiece with her palm. 'I'm glad,' she challenged, 'you told your mother you'd *pacify* me.' She soothed her lips pointedly. Brent smiled cynically at her sarcasm and merely tied his tie. It was her turn then to give him her back to look at. 'Leslie?' She softened her tone. 'Oh dear, yes, I—I had forgotten. That was Mr Napier. I've given him a meal.'

'Call that a meal?' was the mocking rejoinder. 'I'd hardly call it an aperitif.' He was pulling on his jacket. 'Wait until you feel the full impact of my appetite.' He grinned satanically as she mouthed to him to be quiet. With a derisive salute, he left.

'Sorry about that, Leslie. Yes, he's gone. Sorry, too, about forgetting to phone you. I couldn't have made it, anyway.' She listened, then answered, 'Jenny's fretful? Maybe she's still missing her mother.' It was not, she realised, a very tactful remark, but they were the first words that had come into her head. She was still reeling from Brent's kiss. 'Yes, see you tomorrow, both of you.'

She rang off and stood with her hand to her head. There was the clearing away to be done, the dishes to wash—well, it would be tackled tonight. One thing she refused ever to do was to leave today's mess on the doorstep of tomorrow.

When at last she pulled the bedcovers over her, she felt as exhausted as if she had entertained a dozen guests single-handed. Brent, she thought drowsily—it was his fault for kissing her, touching her, taking and taking again without giving a thought to her feelings.

Something disturbed her dream. A noise, a creak or two, a door opening, a key turning . . . A key—no one but Brent had a key to the cottage besides herself. Had he forgotten something? His case, maybe? Or was it an intruder?

Her own door creaked as she opened it carefully. Then she was looking straight into the upraised eyes of Brent Napier. He was holding two suitcases. Under his arms were box files and folders. 'What are you doing here at this time of night?' she whispered, unable to believe her eyes.

He deposited his belongings on the floor and pushed his

fingers into his waistband. 'I've come to rape you this time,' he cracked. 'Abduction had its moments of enjoyment, but there's nothing so gratifying to a man's sense of power over a woman as r-rape.' He rolled the word around his tongue and came two at a time up the wooden stairs.

Linette backed into her bedroom, but he followed her in. 'For—for heaven's sake, Brent!' she faltered, and shrieked as he scooped her up bodily and dropped her bouncing on to the bed. She shook her head frantically. 'You can't—you mustn't . . .'

He switched on the bedside lamp and smiled maliciously, his hand thrust into his trouser pockets. 'What would you do if I did? What could you do? Nothing, witch, absolutely nothing.'

Her head moved from side to side on the pillow. 'Nothing,' she echoed, staring at him, wishing yet again she could judge what his next move might be.

He returned her stare. His expression grew serious, his eyelids flickered like a twitching curtain. If only she could see beyond them to the very depths of his being, as he seemed to be doing with her. You'd only find rock and beyond that more rock, she reminded herself. All this she'd guessed in the early days of their acquaintance. Why should he have changed since then?

'You want me in your bed?' he asked softly. 'Are you asking me silently, "Make love to me"?'

Her lips pressed together and she turned her head away. 'There would be no love, Brent, only lust, and to me, that would be terrible.'

'So you love the man Dickins.' It was a statement. 'Don't try to deny the depth of your relationship with him. I saw that light—this light—on in here for hours.'

She looked at him, unable to defend herself. Hadn't she encouraged him to believe his own construction of how she and Leslie had spent that evening?

'You haven't told me yet why you've come back,' she said.

'For a week or so now, the workmen have been asking

me to get out of my rooms in the house. They want to get on with their work. So, since Mary will be away for a while and you've got a spare room, I decided to accept your hospitality and move in.' His smile baited and she sighed.

'It's the wrong time of day for me to find any smart answers, Brent. It's your cottage. You're at liberty to move in or out of it at will, aren't you? After all, you may call me your tenant, but in law, since I don't pay rent, I'm really your guest.'

He jingled coins in his pocket. He looked her over, first at, then through, her thin nightgown. 'One day you'll pay me,' he mused, 'in full. A lump sum payment.' He bent down, whispering against her lips, 'A night in my arms, witch.'

His kiss was firm but undemanding. His moulding touch, however, aroused in her a response which alarmed her with its potency. She did battle with her reason to hold back and, lemming-like, followed her instincts instead, acknowledging even as she did so that this way, for her, lay only misery and rejection.

Her arms lifted and linked round his neck. She parted her lips, knowingly yet dangerously asking for 'more, please, more.' Brent dropped to the side of the bed, taking over her mouth, which she willingly gave. If only, she thought hazily, she didn't love this man so much. If only his kisses and his deliberate arousal of her desires implied love on his part.

At last, his head lifted and she saw in his eyes a concentration of male need which frightened her. 'Is this the night you pay?' he asked. 'Will you give me what I want?'

'Brent, please understand.' There was a pleading in her eyes which gave him his answer. He thrust her aside and stood up.

'I called you a cheat and you're playing the same game now. I warn you, don't play it too often. My patience isn't limitless, nor are my needs easily quietened once encouraged and aroused. Boy-friend or no boy-friend, I'll

take you, little cheat. And one more thing,' he was at the
door, 'when I do, I vow you'll never forget me. Whoever
you marry, the night you spend with me will haunt you for
the rest of your life.'

The night seemed long, but Linette slept at last. Her alarm
awoke her relentlessly at the usual time and she dragged
herself out of bed. Throwing a wrap round her shoulders,
she went to the bathroom to wash. She tried the handle
and, to her astonishment, found it occupied.

The door was unlocked and opened. Brent was standing
at the mirror, shaving. He was bare to the waist and
Linette's eyes were drawn and caught by the muscled
leanness of him. The urge to touch him was so strong she
had to clasp her hands to make them behave.

He was smiling into the mirror and she realised he could
see her reflection behind him. 'You look pale,' he said,
without altering his expression. 'Anything wrong?'

She drew her wrap more tightly around her. 'I had a
restless night.'

'You did?' he asked in a mock solicitous tone. 'Why was
that?'

'You know very well why.'

A quick turn of his head brought his faintly jeering smile
towards her. 'I left you unsatisfied? Maybe I should have
taken my payment, after all.'

'If only I had a job,' she muttered, 'I'd pay you rent,
then you couldn't make your threats.'

'I'll give you a job.'

'You will?' Her bright eyes found his in the mirror. 'In
your company, you mean? I can type——'

'Right here, in this cottage. As my housekeeper until
Mary comes back.'

She shouldn't have taken his offer seriously. Then the
significance of his statement hit her. 'You'll be staying
here some time?'

'I'll be going abroad very soon. The Napier
Pharmaceuticals division has connections in Holland.

Also, as I said, I'll be flying to Frankfurt. Until then, the answer to your question is "yes".' He grinned. 'Thanks.'

'But I haven't agreed yet.'

'You will.' He dried his face with a towel and walked up to her. 'Kiss me good morning.'

'No. Why should I? I'm not your wife, nor your woman.'

'You're almost that.'

Linette coloured at the truth half-buried beneath the taunt. She turned to go. 'I'll come back when you're finished.'

'No, you don't.' He caught at her wrap which, with no belt to secure it, came open as he pulled her back. 'Come on, kiss me.'

His eyes were laughing, his full lips, with a layer of moisture on the upper one, waited. She wanted to throw herself at him. Instead, she stood on her toes and placed a kiss on the soft dampness.

'What do you call that?' His arm crushed her to him. The feel of his body the length of her made her come alive with a stirring need of him. His kiss was full-bodied, like a heady wine. Like alcohol on an empty stomach, it went straight to her head.

Her body swayed towards him and she felt the caressing roughness of his chest hair, the warmth of his rising desire. When he released her mouth she leant against him.

'Brent, oh, Brent,' she sighed, hearing the note of despair in her own voice. Every day she was falling a little more in love with him—if that were possible. Where would it lead, this unwanted devotion to a man who had no interest in a woman except for the passing pleasure she gave him?

'I'm finished here,' he told her. 'The bathroom's all yours.'

This morning, she decided, I'll wear a dress. She acknowledged her motive. Why try to hide it from herself? She was out to gain his appreciation of her as a woman. As she hurried down the stairs, she knew she had wasted her time. He did not even look at her. There was a smell of toast, and he sat crunching it as if to fill in time.

'Bacon, eggs, tomatoes?' she asked, trying desperately to fulfil her new role as his housekeeper. Only in that way would she have a weapon to wield the next time he talked about 'payment'.

'Cereal, toast, and coffee. I've made the toast.' His quick smile caused her heart to skip. 'My needs are simple. And basic.' He gave her appearance a split-second assessment, then returned to the typewritten sheet he was reading.

Linette's sigh was heartfelt. There was no hurried cooking to be done. 'You're easy to please.'

Again the swift, male appraisal. 'I wouldn't say that. You wouldn't be every man's cup of tea, but you could be mine.' She threatened to throw a cereal packet at him. 'Trouble is,' he emerged from the cover of his upraised arm, 'you keep giving me little sips, when what I really want to do is swallow you down, right down.' There was a touch of lust in his look as it meandered over her. 'I could really gorge myself on you.'

A hand towel flew through the air, hitting him. He emerged from its folds and handed it back.

He smiled broadly. 'If I gave you a ring, would you oblige?'

Her hand shook as she poured his coffee. He wasn't—he couldn't be—serious? Her safest response, she decided, would be to treat it as a joke. 'Tenants don't marry their landlords.'

'They do if it means keeping a roof over their heads.'

With a clatter, she put the pot down. 'Is that a threat?'

'Take it how you like.' Brent's eyes had gone cold. He swallowed his coffee and pushed back his chair.

Dismayed, she watched him gather his belongings. Her impulse was to go to him, make a play of straightening his tie and put her face up for his kiss.

'Are you going?' she asked.

'What does it look like?'

'To London?'

He shook his head. He was a changed man, plunged in

mind if not body into his business world. 'Napier Agricultural Chemicals has an office in Oxford, which is where I'm going. I'll be back this evening.' He stopped near the door. 'I wasn't talking about marriage.'

Her face paled. 'You know how to hand out punches where they hurt most!'

'Don't try to fool me into believing you're the marrying kind.'

There was a hammering and the ring of excited young voices. In the background came the crunch of tyres on gravel. The play-group members were arriving and she hadn't even cleared the breakfast things!

Brent opened the door and watched as, one by one, the little forms came flying in, flinging their arms about Linette's neck. Last of all came Jenny, with Leslie lingering.

'She's still fretful,' he said.

Linette hugged her. 'Not very bright, pet?' she asked.

Jenny shook her head. 'Wish you were my mummy,' she mumbled.

Worried eyes lifted to Leslie's. 'She doesn't mean it.'

'She does,' Leslie asserted doggedly.

Linette looked at Brent, who had not moved. The icy glare of his eyes made frost-bitten fingers walk down her spine. He swung away and was gone.

That afternoon she decided to plan the back garden. It was, in fact, a fenced-in area which was part of the Wealden Grange estate.

There was already a plan in her mind, and with a spade which she found in a small wooden shed, she marked out the beds which would one day be filled with flowers. Over there, she decided, she would have a vegetable patch. It hit her then that her subconscious mind was playing tricks, making her plan into the future. Somehow she would have to tell it that whatever she might plant right now, she would not be there to appreciate the fruits of her efforts.

As the evening approached, her spirits rose. She would

cook something special for Brent's meal. When the play-group had gone that morning, she had dashed to the shops to buy the ingredients to make a spaghetti bolognaise. Now she set about making it, delighting in the fact that she had someone to cook for. The air was filled with the bub-bling smell of the meal in the oven, stimulating the taste buds. Consulting her watch, she tried to estimate the time of Brent's arrival. Since his destination today had been nearer than London, she reasoned that it could well be earlier than last night.

Having set the table for two, she hurried to her bedroom to change. The dress she chose was a lavender blue, with a high-buttoned neckline and shiny matching belt. Her hair sprang with crackling life, dark brown and curling.

There was the sound of a car, striding footsteps and a key in the door. Half-way down the stairs, Linette watched as Brent stood back and motioned to Nita Cutler to precede him into the cottage.

Linette could not hide her dismay. Brent smiled up at her, seeming to notice only the aroma of her lovingly-cooked meal. I cooked it for him, she fumed silently, only for him, not for his woman. A smile curved her mouth, but she knew that a robot might have exhibited more welcome.

Nita nodded, her expression aloof. 'I understand you're acting as Brent's temporary housekeeper.' She breathed in deeply. 'Smells as though he's got himself a cook, too.' Her smile came and went like an artist's lightning sketch, only to be erased as wrong. 'Did you know I was coming?'

'Nobody told me.' She looked accusingly at Brent. 'Nobody phoned.'

Brent deposited his case and peeled off his jacket. 'I'm going to wash. Would you like to go up first, Nita?'

'I'll wait, thanks,' she glanced around, 'make myself comfortable. I could do with a drink.'

'Linette?' Brent had stopped on the stairs.

A hand went to her cheek. That was the one thing she had forgotten! Anyway, she wouldn't have had sufficient money. 'Not a drop—sorry.'

'My God,' Nita groaned, crossing her neat-ankled legs as she sat in a chair, 'so it's to be a teetotal evening. How will I stand it?'

Linette smiled sweetly at Brent, who still hovered. 'Would you like me to run round to the off-licence, Mr Napier? It will only take me about half an hour there and half an hour back. That is, if Miss Cutler can wait that long.'

'Don't be a fool!'

His voice had a harsh edge and she compressed her lips, turning away towards the kitchen. 'Linette!'

'That's okay, Brent,' she hit back, 'I've got a very thick skin. I don't take offence easily.'

'My, my,' Nita murmured, 'my, oh my, Brent! You've got yourself a load of trouble there. I should advertise for an older woman, if I were you. They're usually more respectful.' Her chuckle acted on Linette's nervous system like sandpaper on a polished table. The shine in her eyes was scrubbed out.

Clattering dishes in the kitchen, Linette heard one set of footsteps descend, while another climbed. Brent propped himself against the kitchen door. 'You've set the table for two. Which two?' he asked.

'You and Miss Cutler. Who else?'

'Which means that, since I didn't phone you to tell you I was bringing a guest, you must have used telepathy to tune into my thought waves,' he commented sarcastically. 'You must tell me how you do it some time.' She continued with her work. 'Set yourself a place at the table.'

'No, thank you.' She hoped her tone would freeze him. 'You can't seriously expect me to eat with you and your—friend.' She hoped also that he would notice the hesitation.

He made no response, so she had to look at him to guess whether he did. Even that gave her no answer. 'You heard what I said,' he persisted quietly.

'Mr Napier, I'm your housekeeper—your description. My services are given in lieu of that—that payment you keep demanding. So,' her eyes defied him, 'I shall not set a place for myself. No housekeeper would dream of doing so. And I refuse to give you a weapon to keep wielding in your demand for "payment".'

Still he did not move.

'I'll eat here at the breakfast bar. Now, Mr Napier, if you and your guest are ready for me to serve the meal——'

'Brent darling, which place is mine?' Nita's voice cut off Linette's words.

Brent was beside Linette in a stride. He put his lips against her ear. 'Drop the "Mr". The name's Brent.'

'Yes, Mr Napier.'

His hand grasped a bunch of curls, twisted them and pulled. His mouth stifled her shriek with a deep, hurtful kiss. Her eyes widened in a mute accusation which did not move him at all.

Each time she emerged to serve another portion, the conversation between Brent and his girl-friend came to a stop. Her spirit rebelled against it, but, having put herself into the category of a domestic employee, she told herself she could not complain.

The faintly mocking uprising of Brent's brows exacerbated her inner mutiny, but she kept complete control of her reflexes. Again she reminded herself that she was providing her services in place of the rent he refused to take. When the meal was over and coffee was being poured, she congratulated herself on passing with full marks the test she had set herself.

As she cleared the dishes, the conversation over coffee had turned to business matters. Nita Cutler spoke with fluent authority and an apparent command of her subject which had stark jealousy clawing at Linette's nerves. The woman had the lot, beauty, intelligence—and Brent Napier!

Every kiss he had given her, Linette, had been like tossing a dog a juicy bone. He would have had to have been insensitive beyond belief not to know how his kisses pleased and aroused her. To keep her happy, she fumed, crashing the dishes in the sink, he had made love to her.

While to her it meant the world—she guessed he knew this—to him it had no meaning except the immediate gratification of a passing, and very masculine, need. And yet he had called *her* a cheat.

'Want any help?'

At the sound of his voice behind her, she dashed with the back of her wrist at the moisture brimming from her eyes. Afraid that her voice might waver, she shook her head. When she heard his footsteps recede, the sense of disappointment was hard to bear.

As she passed through the living-room on her way to the stairs, she said tonelessly, 'Good night, Mr Napier, Miss Cutler.'

Brent was spreading papers over the couch while Nita sat forward, hands clasped, plainly interested in the discussion. Brent looked up. 'Where are you going?'

'To my room, Mr Napier,' was her purposely prim answer, hoping it would annoy him.

The lift of his shoulders was a dismissal that wounded, as he must have guessed it would. Nita's smile left her eyes untouched. 'Thank you for the meal, Miss Kemp,' she said. 'It was delicious.'

'Yes, it was, wasn't it?' Linette replied before she could prevent herself, only to receive a cutting look from Brent.

In her bedroom, she tried to read, but the words made no sense. The radio played pleasant music, but its occasional sentimentality threatened to make her tearful again—although, she argued, why she had ever allowed her hopes to be raised by Brent's kisses and intimate caresses, she could not understand.

Restless and feeling caged, she decided to wash her hair. This she did, letting it dry freely. It coiled into tight curls above her shoulders, tangling as the comb snagged its way through them. Since it was still too early for bed, she followed the hair-wash with a bath. Drying herself, she pulled on the bathrobe which hung on the back of the door.

As she let herself out, she stopped short at the sight of Nita going into Brent's bedroom. Brent was at the top of the stairs and Linette found herself face to face with him. His expression was blank, but his eyes were busy flicking over her from curling hair to curling toes.

Her stony gaze bounced off him as he made to move past her.

'Excuse me, please,' he said distantly. She moved back and he went after Nita. Linette did not wait to watch the door close. She fled to her own room and leaned back against the time-grooved wood. I should have known, she thought, swallowing back the misery of seeing her worst fears fulfilled.

Pulling on her nightdress, she swung into bed, overtaken not by misery but by a nagging anger. Her body was tense as her emotions fought a battle with her common sense. She told herself that she knew the score—that Brent and Nita Cutler were of the same world, thought nothing of the occasional night together and, in the morning, waved goodbye, until next time.

Hadn't she fooled Brent into believing that this was the situation between herself and Leslie Dickins? Therefore, her reason argued, she had no right to be thrown so off balance by seeing them enter the same bedroom. No doubt they were this very minute proceeding to make calculated, sophisticated and completely passionless love to each other.

The very thought conjured pictures she could not bear. Frantic fingers pulled the covers over her head, leaving only sufficient space for air to enter. Thus she relaxed slowly and slipped into a troubled sleep. It lasted for about an hour. The cottage was dark and silent when she awoke. The call of a night bird must have awakened her.

Her mouth felt dry and her lips were cracked. The other two occupants of the cottage were either still making tireless love, or were deeply asleep in each other's arms. Either way, they would not hear if she crept downstairs, pocket torch providing a small circle of light, to the kitchen.

She reached the last of the creaking stair treads and turned sharp left. It was then a clear walk through. Her foot coming up against an object tripped her up and forced a strangled shriek from her throat. Her landing place was not the floor as she had anticipated but soft and warm, yet angled and hard at the same time.

'Oh!' she exclaimed with vexation, wounded pride and faint twinges of pain.

'What the hell——?' a smothered voice muttered. He seemed to be fighting free of hair in his mouth. 'Nita?'

'No, I'm not Nita, nor any other of your females. I'm me,' Linette hissed, trying to free herself from trapping arms.

There was a long-suffering groan. 'I might have known,' sighed Brent. 'Trust you to wake me up! Everyone else would carry a torch in the dark, but you——'

'I did! It flew out of my hand and went out.'

'I'm not surprised it went out. You'd drive anybody out—out of their minds!'

'Thanks—thanks a lot,' she replied tearfully, and struggling with the enveloping folds of what appeared to be a blanket. 'How was I to know you were lying here? I thought you were sleeping with Miss Cutler. I saw you go into her room, or rather, your room.'

'Oh, did you?' He had tugged the rug free and had moved on to his side. He pulled her beside him to share the cushions from the settee which formed his bed. 'You've got the impudence to assume that I fall into bed with every woman I bring home? You should have waited, shouldn't you, until you saw me come out again—with this blanket.' He settled himself more comfortably. 'Well now, this time you fell into *my* bed, and of that,' he spoke crisply, 'I intend to take full advantage.'

'Oh no, you won't!' Her legs made prodding contact with his, only to get the worst of the encounter against the hardness of his bones. Her gripping hands pushed at his shoulders which, she found to her dismay, were bare. Was he wearing nothing, then? Her struggles increased to no avail, since he used the easiest remedy of all. He placed himself on top of her.

He found her hands and lifted them to the pillow, one each side of her head. Thus imprisoned, she was helpless. She knew by now that he was wearing one garment—his underpants. Nevertheless, she was aware at once of his arousing desire. This worried her, since she felt within herself an answering desire springing to life.

There was no will inside her now to renew her fight. Brent's face hovered over hers, but the darkness made a secret of his expression. His lips lowered. They were gentle, cooling the atmosphere between them, but tormenting all the same. Linette longed to snuggle up to him, telling him she loved him but—what would be the use?

His current girl-friend was upstairs. Why he had chosen to sleep down here and not with her, she might never know, but she could not—would not allow him to use her as a substitute.

'You've gone cool on me,' he said against her ear. She shivered at his touch, wishing the muscled heaviness of his thighs was not pressing so demandingly on hers.

'I'm tired,' she told him. Her voice had gone thin with her efforts to dowse with cold reason the passion his near-ness excited within her throbbing body.

To her immense relief, he moved on to his side, curling her into him, her back to his front. His seeking hand crept through the unbuttoned opening of her nightdress and found the softness of a breast.

'No, Brent,' she responded, her voice catching.

'Give a man comfort, sweetheart. Let me take the softness of you into my dreams.'

'I—I should go back to bed, Brent.'

'You should be here, by my side. Now, share my bed, such as it is, and share my sleep, too.' He nuzzled the back of her neck. 'Did I remember to tell you how much I love your body?'

My body, she thought, not me! Or was he imagining she

was Nita, as Leslie, when he kissed her, imagined she was Jane, his estranged wife? What did it matter? she asked, drifting into sleep at last. The magic of his arm about her, his hand holding her so intimately, gave a brilliance of colour to her dreams that she knew she would never experience again.

# CHAPTER NINE

WAKING with a start, it took a few seconds for her to realise she was not in her own bed and that she was alone. When she saw where she had spent the night, she held her cheeks in horror. Had she really lain there, beside Brent, with his woman guest asleep upstairs?

Where was that guest now? Linette listened with concentration, hearing nothing but the birds outside and the faint sound of cars driving on the main road which ran past her uncle's cottage.

It could only mean, she concluded, rising hurriedly and gathering the scattered cushions, that Nita Cutler had left with Brent. They must have crept about in order to avoid waking her. But how had they cooked their breakfasts without making a clatter?

Putting the folded rug and pillows into a pile, Linette went into the kitchen. It was exactly as she had left it last night. It meant that they had dressed, washed and gone without bothering to make even a cup of coffee. She blushed to imagine how Nita must have laughed at the whole situation—and how Brent must have joined in— after they had got into Brent's car.

Hurrying upstairs to dress, she went first to Brent's bedroom, changing and tidying the bed. Then she raced to her own room, dressing quickly before washing. It was as she combed her hair that she saw on the small chest beneath the mirror a note propped against an envelope.

With shaking fingers, she opened it, recognising the handwriting at once. 'Please find enclosed in the envelope,' Linette read, 'a solution to the cash-flow problem you must be experiencing as a result of buying food to feed my guest and myself. I have ordered a selection of frozen foods to be delivered to you later today. Your uncle has promised to provide you with all the vegetables you need.' It was signed, Brent Napier.

The signature, like the note itself, was coldly formal.

Indignation told her to reject the notes, but cold reason made her admit that she needed the money. Wearing her oldest clothes, she started to put into a practical form the plans she had made in her mind for the creation of a back garden.

As she dug the earth, the cool tone of Brent's note taunted her. Where had he gone with Nita Cutler? Back to Oxford, or to the London headquarters? Would he come home for a meal? If so, what time? All right, so she was acting like an anxious wife, which she had no right to do, but he had appointed her his housekeeper, and even a housekeeper needed to know such things.

It was towards the end of the afternoon that the phone call came. Linette raced in from the garden, her hand shaking as she answered it. Her excitement ended as a woman's voice enquired whether she was Miss Kemp, Mr Napier's housekeeper.

'I'm Mr Napier's secretary,' the woman went on, 'I'm calling you from our London office at Mr Napier's request. He won't be home for a couple of weeks, Miss Kemp. He's just left for Frankfurt.'

'I see,' Linette managed, hoping she sounded like an efficient housekeeper. 'He did mention something about going abroad, though he didn't say when. Thank you for telling me.'

'That's quite all right,' the woman responded obligingly. 'Oh, and one other thing. He asked me to say thank you for all the home comforts you gave him, which he realises were outside your normal duties. He also hopes the financial situation has been temporarily relieved.' The woman gave a little laugh. 'I really don't know what he's talking about, but I expect you do.'

'Oh, yes, I certainly do,' Linette came back grimly. Softening her tone and hoping she had not offended the woman when it was the man at whom her sharpness should be aimed, she repeated, 'Thank you for phoning me,' and rang off.

The days stretched ahead like a desert without an oasis. She wandered from room to room, looking at each piece of furniture, every shadowed corner, every wall, as if she had never seen them before. Her mind was looking inward and it found a wilderness there, too. What would she do without him? Would she listen for his key each evening, cook for two by mistake, only to throw it all away because she had lost her appetite?

What, she wondered miserably, staring out at the half-dug garden, would she do for the rest of her life, when he was gone from it completely? She had never known, no one had ever told her, that it was possible to love someone so completely you felt half dead when that person wasn't there.

Was this how her uncle felt when his wife—her aunt—had died? If so, no wonder he had grown so taciturn in recent years. Yet he had never said a word to anyone about his private feelings.

How had she let herself fall into the trap of Brent Napier's charms, especially when it had been his sole aim in life to get her out of his? The phone rang and again she ran to answer. When she heard the voice, she told herself she should have known it wouldn't be Brent.

'Linette?' came the familiar, plaintive question. 'Are you free this evening?'

In her unhappiness, she had forgotten Leslie. He plainly had not forgotten her. 'Hi, Leslie. I'm free as a bird.' She hoped he would not detect the false brightness.

He had not, since he was deep in troubles of his own. 'It's Jenny—I think she's got a fever. Her temperature's high. She seems to have a cold, too. I'm at a loss, Lin. Never had to deal with this sort of thing before.'

'You want me to come round?'

'Yes, please. How soon?' he asked urgently. 'I'll come for you.'

'Come right now,' she answered. 'There's no meal to get ready. Mr Napier's away, so it's only me tonight.' Well, part of me, she thought.

By the time Leslie arrived, Linette had changed her blouse and found a clean pair of jeans. Grabbing a jacket, she hurried down the stairs and opened the entrance door. 'Anything you want me to bring?' she asked him, but he shook his head.

His car was parked outside the gates. As they drove away, Linette asked, 'Is Jenny still fretful?'

'Worse then ever, Lin. She screamed when I came out and I had to trouble the neighbour again.'

Leslie used his key and as soon as they entered his house, he called, 'I'm home, poppet!'

The neighbour came down the stairs with an air of relief. 'Poor wee girl,' she commented. 'You going to look after her, Miss Kemp?' Linette nodded. 'She wants her mummy, that's who she wants, but she won't get.'

'Maybe she'll make do with me,' Linette replied with a weak smile, and trod the stairs with a rising anxiety. When she entered the little girl's room, she knew her worry had been well merited.

Jenny tried a smile, but it soon vanished. Her eyes were red, as were her cheeks and forehead, which burned under Linette's hand. Now and then a cough shook the small body.

'What do you think?' Leslie asked, his eyes heavy as if he had not slept.

'I'm wondering,' Linette ventured, holding the pale, lifeless hand which lay on the covers, 'if it's measles. Mary, who cooks and cleans for Mr Napier, is off work looking after one of her children. He's got measles.'

Leslie nodded. 'I heard it's just started to go round the village.'

'Have you called the doctor?' Leslie shook his head. 'You'd better phone him at once, Leslie.'

Like a child in a situation beyond its control, he hurried down the stairs to the telephone. The doctor came, confirmed Linette's diagnosis, wrote a prescription and after giving instructions regarding treatment, left. He had assumed that Linette was Leslie's wife, and she did not have the heart to enlighten him.

Two hours later, Linette had cooked a meal for Leslie and herself, given Jenny innumerable drinks and sat at her bedside. As she washed Jenny's face, she noticed that one or two spots were already appearing. They were, she knew, the first of the many to come.

Staying until Jenny slept, she told Leslie she would have to go. With reluctance, he agreed, and took her home. 'Will you come tomorrow?' he asked eagerly. 'I could get time off work, but——'

'I'll come. The play-group will have to be cancelled, anyway. I suspect the mothers won't want their children to mix too closely with this going around.'

Next morning, Linette phoned the homes of the play-group children. The mothers sounded relieved, as if the problem had been resolved for them. Linette spent the rest of the day at Leslie's house, taking over once again from the neighbour.

Leslie came home heavy-eyed and worried. 'I hardly got a wink of sleep last night, Lin—Jenny kept calling me. In the end I sat in a chair and dozed.'

'She's slept a bit during the day,' Linette told him, 'but she's run me off my feet, I must admit.' She added a tired smile.

'You're so good,' Leslie told her. 'I don't know how to thank you.'

'Don't bother. Leslie?'

'Mm?' He sank into a chair, pale-faced and despairing.

'Would you like me to stay the night? I see you've got a spare bed.'

He brightened at once. 'Would you, Lin? I didn't like to ask.'

'There's nothing at the cottage to rush home for.' She realised how disconsolate she sounded, but knew Leslie would not pick it up. 'At least you'd get a good night's sleep so that you can face work tomorrow.'

When the evening meal had been cleared and Jenny had settled down, if not for the night, then for a few hours, Linette remembered that she should let her uncle know where she was.

Mrs Napier answered. 'You're where, dear?' Linette repeated the information. 'I see. And you're staying the night?'

'Maybe one or two, Mrs Napier. Jenny's so miserable she keeps waking up, so I thought I'd give Leslie a break——'

'I understand, Linette. I remember how badly it affected Brent all those years ago. Then his younger sister caught it and I was nearly dropping with fatigue.'

'I didn't know Brent had two sisters,' Linette put in.

'He hasn't told you? Just like a brother! Her name is Marion and she lives with her husband and family in New Zealand.'

'Brent's secretary phoned me this morning. Brent's gone abroad, she said.'

'That's right. He's in Germany now, then he goes to Switzerland for a few days, then a quick call at the offices of one of our subsidiary companies in Amsterdam. All that travelling—it means nothing to him.'

Linette laughed, assuming that that was what she was expected to do. In reality, she felt like crying. So many days without a sight of him . . .

'Uncle Godfrey—he's all right?'

'He's just fine, dear. He's in the garden—where else would he be? Which is why I answered your call. He told me he doesn't like speaking on the telephone.'

Linette laughed again, genuinely this time. 'I think he's secretly afraid of it.'

Mrs Napier chuckled. 'Well, I hope the dear little girl is better soon. Now you mustn't go overdoing things, Linette. I'll explain to your uncle.'

'And give him my love. 'Bye, Mrs Napier.'

Linette sat in a chair and took the cup of tea which Leslie had made. Feeling too tired to make conversation, she drank the warming liquid, staring through the window at nothing. Leslie fidgeted, poured himself a second cup, took a few mouthfuls and spoke at last.

'There's a rumour——' he paused as if questioning his own common sense in mentioning the subject, but persisted, 'going around that you and—Mr Napier are——' He stopped.

'Are what, Leslie?' Linette pressed, her heart already drumming in anticipation.

'Are living together.'

'Really?' She put down her cup, having to gather her wits. 'Well, we are, aren't we? Sharing the same cottage, I mean.' She looked at him. 'Do you believe—what other people believe?'

'Knowing you, Lin, I don't—really.'

'You mean you've got your doubts.' He was shaking his head, but she snapped, 'Well, they're wrong, all of them. He moved in because the builders had reached his rooms at the Grange.'

Leslie nodded vigorously. 'But people do say——' He hesitated again. 'They say you've been seen kissing in public.'

Linette's mind sped back to the occasion when Brent had taken her to a more distant country pub and the gossiping local woman had spoken to her about Brent. He had kissed her out of devilment. How could she explain that to Leslie? And why should she?

'So he kissed me. What's a kiss?' It hurt her merely to say the words. 'Don't try and equate me with your wife, Leslie. If I married a man—and no one's even asked me— I'd stick with him through heaven and hell. If—if there

were anything between myself and Brent—and there's
not——'

Well, there wasn't, she told herself severely. Remember
that cold little note.

'It would be our business, wouldn't it?' she continued.
'He's free and I'm free, and if anyone mentions the rumour
to you, I'd be delighted if you'd tell them just that.'

'Yes, yes, I understand, but I thought I should mention
it.'

'Thanks, Leslie. Anyway, he's got a woman. Her name's
Nita Cutler. She's beautiful and sophisticated and she's
got everything.' Her voice had gone flat.

Leslie yawned and at once apologised. 'It's the disturbed
night,' he said unnecessarily.

'Go up, Leslie,' Linette urged. 'If Jenny wakes, I'll go to
her. I don't mind, honestly,' as Leslie was about to protest.
'That's why I'm staying.'

He thanked her and told her where to find towels, a new
toothbrush and everything else she might need. 'A nightdress—do you wear——?'

Solemnly, Linette nodded, suppressing a smile at Leslie's
embarrassment. And had this man once asked her to come
and live with him? 'Okay if I borrow one of your wife's?'

He explained where she would find one and gladly went
up to bed. Soon afterwards Linette followed him, deciding
to get some sleep while Jenny was quiet.

Linette stayed for nearly two weeks, seeing Jenny
through the worst of the illness. When Leslie felt he could
cope, Linette went home. Jenny hugged her desperately,
not wanting her to go. Linette explained that while her
daddy was out, the lady next door would look after her,
but still Jenny cried. Linette detached herself with a firmness painful even to herself and said she would call in next
day.

On her way home, she went to see her uncle. Aileen
Napier opened the door, her face as bright as it ever was.
'Your uncle's in his usual place.' She closed the door.
'We're so glad you've called, Linette. Do come in.' There

was a subdued excitement in her voice which brought a curious frown to Linette's face.

'Hallo, lass,' said Godfrey, making a show of rising. This deepened Linette's frown. Never before had she known her uncle observe such social niceties. His sub-tenant's influence, she thought with amusement, must have been greater than she could ever have imagined.

'Oh dear, Linette,' Aileen Napier remarked, 'how tired you look. Do sit down before you fall down. How is the little girl?'

'Much better, thanks,' Linette told her, 'but she didn't want me to go.'

'From the sound of it,' came the gruff voice of her uncle, 'nor did the child's father.'

Linette swung towards him. 'What do you mean, Uncle?'

'Snappy, are you? Well, I'm only going by the rumour that's going round about you and this Leslie Dickins. He's her father, isn't he? You've stayed there a couple of weeks. What else do you expect people to think?'

'Another rumour? First, it's Brent and me, now it's Leslie and me. Uncle,' she turned to him despairingly, 'you don't mean you've been taken in, too? You know me better than that. I went there to look after his child who was ill, and that's just what I did. Uncle Godfrey, how could you?'

'No need to shout your head off at me, lass. I had to test you, didn't I? I knew if it wasn't true you'd bite my head off.'

'Then it's a good thing you're not both headless,' Mrs Napier remarked, at which Linette laughed, then collapsed into the armchair in tears.

'Now look what you've done, Godfrey,' Aileen scolded, putting her arm round Linette's shoulders.

'It's all the strain,' he commented wisely. 'It had to come out. Better here than on her own.'

'You old devil, Godfrey Barker!'

'Now, Aileen, don't talk to your future husband like that!'

Linette stopped crying as if a switch had been flipped.

She lifted her head and stared out of dark, tear-brimmed eyes. 'What did you say?'

'We meant it to be a lovely surprise, but—well, get out your hankie, dear, and mop up.'

Linette obeyed, then stared first at one, then the other. 'You mean you're getting married? You and Uncle Godfrey?' At last it registered, and Linette broke the incredulous silence. 'But that's great, that's wonderful! I'm so glad, so happy for both of you. Congratulations—and how did it happen?' There was laughter at this and Linette, her tears dry, stood up.

First she hugged her uncle, then more shyly, put a kiss on Aileen Napier's cheek.

'It—well, it just happened,' Aileen explained. 'We thought it would be a good idea. We were getting along so well, working together, living together—and not in the way your generation would mean, young lady.' She smiled mischievously at Linette, who laughed.

'And you, Uncle?'

'It was like Aileen said,' was all Linette could get out of him.

Aileen had bought some wine—not too expensive, she informed them, but good all the same. They drank toasts to each other, then Linette toasted the newly-engaged couple.

Her tiredness hit her again and Aileen noticed, bundling her down the road back home. Godfrey stood beside the woman he was soon to marry and waved his niece most of the way back.

It was when she let herself into the cold and empty cottage that her loneliness hit her, and her eyes went to the telephone wishing it could speak and tell her if Brent had called. There were letters on the mat, but of little consequence. There was not a single communication from him, not a card, not even a short memo such as the one he had left the day he and his girl-friend had departed.

The news she had just heard cheered her, but it would not take away the pain of the continued absence of the man she loved. All right, she talked back to herself, so he didn't love her. That didn't mean she could stop loving him.

With resolution, she pulled on her old clothes. Since there was a restlessness in her limbs which all the reason in the world could not drive out, she would go into the garden and dig until she dropped. That way, maybe she could get some rest.

Fatigue caught up with her and after a light evening meal she slumped into an armchair. Until the programme she wanted to watch came on television, she decided to read. Even this proved impossible. In trying to drive out the restlessness from her extremities, she had propelled it upwards into her brain. Flinging down the magazine, she let her head recline against the chair back.

The next thing she heard was the tinkling chime of the pendulum clock from the other room telling her cheerfully that it was eleven o'clock. Outside it was dark and the blackness made reflectors of the window panes. Starting up, she saw herself dishevelled and staring-eyed with interrupted sleep.

A face appeared against the glass of the window overlooking the front of the cottage. It took a split second for her brain to register that it was not her own, and her hands sprang to hold her cheeks in momentary terror.

It was a woman's face, someone she had never seen before. It disappeared and there came a knocking on the door. With shaking hands, Linette opened the window and called, 'Yes?'

'Are you Miss Kemp, Linette Kemp?' The voice was that of a young woman.

'Yes, that's me. W-why?'

'I want to speak to you.'

'Who are you? I must know before I open the door.'

'You'll know soon enough.'

Taking courage from the fact that there was no menace in the woman's tone, only anger, Linette opened the door slowly. It was pushed against her, but the visitor did not step inside.

Her face was pale, her eyes were underlined by dark shadows. She wore a coat that looked travel-creased and well worn. In better light and happier circumstances she guessed the woman would probably look quite attractive. Her hair was fair . . . the shape of her face not unfamiliar . . . Jenny? Leslie's wife?

'Yes, you might look at me like that, you might look surprised. You know who I am, don't you? Jane Dickins, that's my name.'

Linette could not understand why the woman was so angry. Hadn't she looked after Jenny, her daughter, as devotedly as any mother might? The wavering smile which Linette managed to produce only seemed to make the woman's displeasure increase.

'Don't smile like that at me, Miss Kemp, because I've a mind to wipe it clean off your face!'

Linette fingered the thin gold chain around her neck. 'Why, what have I ever done to you? I'm tired out with nursing your daughter through a nasty attack of measles——'

'Is that what you call it?' Jane Dickins came back, on the verge of hysteria.

'Look, come in, Mrs Dickins. I'll make a cup of tea and we can chat over it.'

'I wouldn't taste a thing you made me, not a thing. And I'm not going to thank you for what you did for Jenny, because of what my neighbour told me.'

Linette frowned. 'What did she tell you, Mrs Dickins?' she asked in a soothing voice.

'That you stayed for twelve nights with my husband, that's what!'

'That's true, but what was wrong with that? Jenny kept waking him. I saved him from all those broken nights by going in to her myself.'

'You slept with him, that's what you did!' The woman was almost screaming now. 'Don't try and deny it—he told me so himself.'

'Leslie told you?' Linette felt in need of a chair, but since the woman would not step over the threshold, she forced her legs to stiffen. 'It was a lie, Mrs Dickins. He only said it to make you——'

The rest of the sentence was lost in an avalanche of abuse. 'I'd decided to come back to him a couple of weeks ago. I wrote to him, but he didn't answer my letter. No wonder he didn't! He was having a good time with you, wasn't he?'

Linette's hand went to her head. She was caught in a web of family warfare. Leslie had used her to make his wife jealous. If this was the way Leslie had found to thank her for all she had done ... but she could not regret one moment of the time she had devoted to helping Jenny recover from her illness. Nor could she blame him, really, for using her, since she had known all along that he still loved his wife and wanted her back.

'Mrs Dickins,' Linette said wearily, 'if you choose to believe that, then I can't stop you. But it isn't true, I swear it isn't true.'

'Of course it isn't true.' The voice came from out of the darkness and the figure of a man loomed, broad, head high, his solid outline materialising from the unlighted darkness beyond.

'Brent?' Linette whispered, delight chasing away her fatigue. 'You're home?'

He was beside her now, his suitcase pushed inside the doorway. 'I'm home, my love.'

Linette rejoiced in his greeting. Had he missed her as desperately as she had missed him? His arm held her closely and he turned to the astounded onlooker. 'You see how my fiancée greets me, Mrs Dickins. Those rumours, as you can judge for yourself, were nonsense.' He looked down at his wide-eyed 'fiancée'. 'You were acting the good Samaritan, weren't you, my love?'

Dumbly, Linette nodded and he placed a fleeting kiss on her upturned lips. 'Looking after Jenny,' she added a little unnecessarily, but too dazed to know what she was saying.

The woman on the doorstep was, it seemed, equally dazed. 'Well,' she said, 'it looks as though Miss Kemp was speaking the truth.' She pushed her fair hair from her eyes. 'I'm sorry if I upset you, Miss Kemp, after all you've done for Jenny. But why did Leslie tell me—what he did tell me?'

Brent's smile was filled with charm. 'Think a moment, Mrs Dickins. Could it have been a trick on his part to make you—jealous?'

Jane Dickins frowned, then a smile broke through. 'You wait till I get home, Mr Napier, I'll tell him what I think of his stories! You are Mr Napier, aren't you?' she queried. 'There were rumours about you and her, too, and now I see—if you don't mind my saying so—those might be right!'

A lifted finger from Brent, smilingly urging her to silence, made the woman laugh.

'So you're engaged, Miss Kemp,' she remarked. 'I'm sure Leslie will be delighted when I tell him.' She could not have seen Linette's doubtful frown. 'Goodnight, then, you two, and——' she looked at Brent, 'and thanks.' Her hurrying form disappeared into the darkness from which Brent had come.

The closing of the door strangely did not warm the atmosphere. Linette shivered slightly as she leaned back against it, yet her eyes were shining as they sought his. Finding them, she saw the reason for her involuntary shiver.

His gaze was at its iciest. Even so, she ventured a smile, saying, 'I'm not really your fiancée, am I, Brent?' She had made the words into a statement, not wishing to be slapped down by letting him believe that in a question there could only be hope on her part.

He answered her with a hooded look, his fingers loosening his tie and removing it. He turned and crossed the room to the wide fireplace, all the while peeling off his jacket and throwing it aside. Hands in pockets, he regarded her, and she knew she did not imagine the contempt in his expression.

Her shaking hand passed across her forehead. The ache there echoed the pain of tiredness—and anti-climax—inside her. In her imaginings, she had felt his arms around her the moment he stepped in the door, her mouth lifting to his whispering that she loved him just before his kiss took her breath, and powers of speech, away.

Congratulating herself on her confident smile, she said, 'You didn't really believe what Jane Dickins was saying.'

His answer came like the blows of a hammer. 'I believed every word.'

'So why did you get me off the hook by telling her I was your fiancée?' she demanded, anger laying a veneer over her tiredness.

'Believe it or not,' he replied coolly, 'I was trying to save their marriage, not your reputation.'

She was more bewildered than angry. 'But, Brent, you must surely know me well enough to realise it just couldn't be true.'

'I haven't forgotten seeing that light in your bedroom the evening he came to visit you. That's evidence enough for me. And,' his long legs brought them face to face, his derisive gaze all over her, tearing her apart, 'I've decided I don't "know" you well enough. As your fiancé, I intend to remedy that before the night is over.'

'You don't know what you're saying.' She felt her legs weaken, her heartbeat hurry with fear.

'I'm stone cold sober, sweetheart. I've driven many miles to see you.' The harshness of his tone robbed the words of all emotion. 'I know what I'm saying. I also know that you're not going to disappoint me after my long journey to see you.'

He bent and swung her into his arms, making for the stairs. 'You're going to bed,' he stated, 'with me.'

Even as his strides took them upwards, the movements of his muscles excited her. The arm she had put around his neck for balance was joined by her other arm and they clung as if to prevent him from ever going away again. If she could tell him how much she had missed him, would that soften his mood?

'Brent, I——' She looked around. 'This isn't my room.'

'I told you, you're sleeping with me.' He dropped her on to the covers and started unfastening his shirt, watching her as he did so. 'Now take your clothes off,' he commanded. 'Or do you want me to tear them off you?'

Linette started up, swinging her feet to the floor. 'You would, too, wouldn't you? Like you let those bailiffs smash my miniatures.'

'I seem to remember I picked up the pieces. This time, I'm damned if I'm going to. And when I've finished with you,' he forced up her chin, adding slowly, 'you'll be shattered.'

Linette made her lips fashion a smile as if she was accepting all he said. Then she dived beneath his arm and raced for the door. Before she could reach it he had caught her, his hand gripping the waistband of her jeans. She doubled over, as if she was winded, hoping he would relent and loosen his hold.

Instead, he urged her backwards. Giving up that tactic, she straightened, only to find the hardness of him against her back. Brent's arms went round her, crossing against her breasts, imprisoning each one in a cupping hand. For a while they stayed this way, then she felt his mouth placing small kisses around the back of her neck. Her skin prickled and her head went back against him.

His tactics had changed and if she was not careful, all her mental strength to fight him would have ebbed. The moment her clawing fingers fought to remove his hands, they were at her waist on their way to her thighs. Now they were moving inwards, their intention plainly being to meet in an intimacy she could not allow.

Swinging round, she scraped her nails down his bared chest. In a second, her wrists were caught in two iron-fingered vices, but she would not give in. Twisting her hands in a bid for freedom, she spat out, 'I want to draw blood—your blood!'

'Oh no, you little vampire, that you won't do.' He released her hands and she went for his chest again, only to discover to her fury that his chest hair acted as a protection from the impact of her nails.

While she had been diverted in her attempts to fulfil her wish, his fingers had been more successful in their aim. All her front buttons were unfastened and her blouse was jerked from her shoulders. It hit the carpet.

'Leave me alone,' she cried, 'I *will not* sleep with you!' She looked down and to her horror her jeans were almost pulled away. Brent lifted her, trod on them and they came off entirely. He swung her round and on to the bed again.

He shed his shirt and went for the buckle of his belt. When she saw he had meant every threat he had made, she swung her legs as if to make another run for it. With ease, he caught her ankles and flung them back on to the covers.

His arm slid under her back and deftly removed her bra. 'No, please,' she pleaded. 'You don't know the truth. What Jane Dickins said was wrong—wrong! I wouldn't sleep with a man—just any man . . .'

'Only a special one,' he sneered, 'and what was Dickins to you if not special?'

'Brent, you must believe me—no, no!' She tried to sit up to prevent him from removing her final barrier, but he held her down with his free hand. Then he stood over her, arms folded, as she lay supine, helpless under the threat of his superior strength and the burning trail of his very male scrutiny.

Whatever move she made now, she would be the loser. If she ran, he would catch her. If she stayed, he would take everything from her, all that she, as a woman, had to give.

Closing her eyes, cold now with utter weariness and an encroaching sense of shock, she let her body go limp. 'You've won, Brent, as you always do. Take from me whatever you want,' she told him tiredly. 'You hold all the cards. I don't have the power to stop you.' She turned her darkly-shadowed eyes up to his. 'But I warn you, you'll hate yourself afterwards. Because, you see,' she gazed steadily up at him, 'it would be rape.'

'Rape? After twelve nights in Dickins' arms? You're so conditioned by now to the role of sleep-around, you'd come if I whistled!'

She gritted her teeth, forcing herself not to hit back at his calculated insults.

'But you're right.' He bent to retrieve his shirt. 'I would hate myself—for following your pet lover, second in line for your favours. You're tainted,' he scorned. 'I wouldn't make love to you now if you were the last woman on earth. Now, get out of my room.' He watched and waited, hands on hips.

Slowly, Linette lifted herself from the bed, crossing her arms in front of her. If she hoped he would relent and give her the clothes he had taken from her, she was disappointed. Unable to rid herself of the feeling of humiliation, she picked up her clothes from the floor and dressed in front of him, then went to the door.

Turning, she said, 'You were right—I'm shattered. But you haven't broken my spirit, so there are no pieces for anyone to pick up, let alone you. I—I loved you, Brent.'

The reaction she expected did not come. He regarded her steadily, not even a flicker in his gaze.

'But not any more. I think I hate you, really hate you for this.'

'As you've said before. To put my point of view as bluntly as you've put yours, I have nothing but contempt for you. I like my women straightforward and honest. Maybe if you'd come clean . . .'

'But I am straightforward and honest,' she flung back, her voice rising. 'And there was nothing to come clean about.' He gave a twisted smile. 'Oh, what's the use?' she finished despairingly, and went with heavy steps to her own room.

# CHAPTER TEN

WHEN Linette dragged herself from bed after her alarm had awoken her, she had the feeling that she was alone in the cottage.

Later, having washed and dressed, she descended the stairs and found that, as she had suspected, Brent had gone. This time there was no note awaiting her, nor, later that morning, did Brent's secretary call her from London with a cryptic message about 'home comforts'.

Just after breakfast the telephone did ring. Although her heart leapt, she told herself not to be foolish. It was her uncle.

'How nice to hear you talking on the telephone, Uncle Godfrey,' she joked as brightly as she could manage.

There was no answering chuckle, but she had not expected one. Nor had she expected a gruff, 'Could you come round, Lin?'

She knew better than to ask him why he wanted her there. 'I'll come straight away.'

When Godfrey opened the door, Linette knew that something was wrong. He walked slowly, head bent, to his favourite chair, motioning her to the chair she used to occupy but which Mrs Napier seemed cheerfully to have taken over.

Linette looked around. 'Where is she? Your betrothed, I mean.' She spoke lightly.

'She's gone—this morning, with her son.' Godfrey stared with unseeing eyes at the opposite window. 'She won't come back.'

All of Linette's own troubles receded under the impact of her uncle's. She was young. She could—just—bear rejection, but her uncle had surely suffered enough. He had lost one woman he had loved. It wasn't fair that he should have the loss of another inflicted on him.

'Why, Uncle, why?' He was silent. 'Tell me,' she urged.

The silence lengthened, and he said at last, 'She worked beside me. She understood me. I understood her—or thought I did. Whatever job she did, she worked hard at. She'd come with me of a night to the pub. She'd talk to my friends just like she was one of us, which I thought she was. Until this morning.'

'What happened this morning, Uncle?' Linette encouraged, her interlinked hands white through tension. 'Nothing to do with Brent and me?'

'Not with you, Lin.'

'Brent? He was mixed up in it?' If he's told his mother about what happened between us, she thought furiously, if he's persuaded her to have nothing to do with the family, I'll—I'll——

'In a way, yes. In another way, no.' His eyes were heavy with despair as they lifted to Linette's. 'She was living a lie. If she'd told me the truth from the start . . .'

Linette schooled herself to wait until her uncle felt able to continue.

'You see,' he explained at last, 'when the postman comes, I'm usually at work out there. Well, this morning there was a shower of rain.'

Was there? Linette wondered. She had been too deeply into her own misery to notice.

'Aileen usually collects the letters—it was an arrangement we had.' He frowned. 'Now I know why.'

'Why, Uncle?' Linette queried patiently.

'I picked them up, you see. There were three, two for her, one for me. It was the name on both of hers that caught my eye.'

Linette held her breath.

'They both said, "Mrs Aileen Napier, Chairman, Napier Agricultural Chemicals Ltd.," then there was my address, with "care of" in front of it.'

Linette struck her fist against her palm. 'I knew she wasn't just the mother-figure she seemed. Right from the start I thought she had a certain air about her that made her different from—well, different,' she finished.

'She's a top executive, Lin, almost as high up as her son.'

'He's the Chief Executive? Of the whole Napier Organisation?'

Godfrey nodded. 'There's a large group of companies, or so she said.'

Linette counted on her fingers. 'Pharmaceuticals, fertilisers, medicinal drugs. I can imagine the rest.' And she had thought he might have grown to love her—a small-town little nobody called Linette Kemp? If she didn't feel like crying, she would have laughed.

'So it's all over, you see.' Her uncle let his head rest back. She saw the worry lines, the laughter lines—there were few enough of those since he rarely laughed.

But Aileen Napier had made him laugh, made him happy—fooled him into feeling enough affection for him to ask her to marry him. And from Uncle Godfrey, that was indeed a compliment.

Linette leaned back in the chair, closed her eyes and tried to think. It was no use, since all that happened was that a face kept appearing—a strong face, its features as full of vitality as the body that went with it.

Shaking her head to make the image go away, she shook in an idea to take its place. She sprang to her feet. 'We're going places, Uncle. We're taking the train to London.'

He struggled from his chair. 'You can go if you want, Lin, but you're not getting me on a journey to that noisy place. I'm staying here, in the peace and quiet of my own home.'

Linette smiled secretly, for she knew better.

On the train, they sat facing each other. Godfrey's face still held a look of rebellion. They were the only two passengers in the carriage.

'You look nice, Uncle, dressed in your best.'

Godfrey looked down at his well-polished shoes, his

Harris tweed jacket and the trousers with their knife-sharp creases which had hung unused in his clothes cupboard for so long. He shrugged as if he didn't care, but Linette knew that, deep down, he was proud of the way he looked.

'Do you think Mrs Napier will admire you so much she'll come back?' Linette asked the question to gauge his reaction.

'Who said I wanted her back?' he demanded belligerently. 'I should never have let you persuade me to come. I'm not running after any woman, begging her to—to marry me.'

By his answer, Linette could guess how deeply affected her uncle had been by Mrs Napier's deceit. He stared out of the window at the passing countryside. Linette looked down at the dark blue jacket and skirt she was wearing. Her top was a simple white blouse. Her reflection in her bedroom mirror had told her she looked like a girl travelling to attend an interview.

Well, she communicated with her ghostly twin looking back at her from the train window, she was, wasn't she? A very important interview—with the head of the entire Napier Organisation. He was the man who had shared her bed, whose bed she had almost shared, with whom she had slept on the floor of the living-room.

He was no stranger to her, this important man. The very thought of him set her nerves tingling and started an ache for his touch for which the only cure was the taste of his love. That, she knew now for certain, was a heady drink which would never pass her lips.

As she worried at the amethyst and gold ring which her parents had given her on her eighteenth birthday, she wondered if she had done the right thing in spending so much money in dragging her uncle to London. Then he started speaking, and she knew she had.

'We talked about it, Lin,' he said, without turning his head from the fields and hills. 'She asked me what difference did it make that she was a director in her son's company. I said it made a lot of difference. That car she drove around in for a start.'

'But I thought that was one of Brent's?'

Godfrey shook his head. 'It was hers.'

He sighed, and Linette waited patiently.

'I told her I couldn't live up to the standards of such a lady,' he went on. 'I wasn't rich. I couldn't give her fine clothes and fancy outings to fancy eating places. A drink and a sandwich in the pub was all right for me.'

'What did she say to that?'

'She said my standards were hers, didn't I know that by now? She said she didn't want fine clothes, she had more than enough of the things to last her a lifetime. She said she didn't go for soft lights and over-polite waiters. She'd had her fill of them to last a lifetime, too.'

'And she said,' Linette took him up, 'that she also loved a drink and a sandwich in a pub. Right?'

Her uncle nodded.

'So what was the problem?'

He shook his head as if that problem was much too large for a man such as he was to explain. 'I just couldn't live up to her,' he repeated unhappily.

'Do you still want her to marry you, Uncle?'

Godfrey lifted his shoulders and let them fall. He changed the subject. 'Will you set up the stall tomorrow, Lin, like you used to do?'

'Get your breakfast and make your bed and all the rest?' she teased, hoping to divert him a little.

He nodded, brushing imaginary mud from his spotless trousers. Mud and Aileen Napier, she could almost hear him thinking—they just didn't go together any more.

They had a sandwich lunch at the mainline station buffet, then found their way with some difficulty to High Holborn, emerging from the Underground station into the sunshine. There was no need to ask the way to the offices of the Napier Company. They towered above most of the other buildings and seemed, to Godfrey's dazed eyes, to be made almost entirely of glass.

A short walk brought them to the glass swing doors.

Godfrey tugged at his niece's arm. 'You're not getting me in there.'

'Uncle,' she said with mock severity, 'we haven't come all this way only to turn around when we get here and go home. Come on, where's your courage?'

Firmly she linked her arm in his, pushed the door with an air of confidence she certainly did not feel, and released him. He seemed too scared to take another step.

Linette walked, straight-backed, to the enquiries desk. There were four receptionists on duty. One was free. Linette stated, head high, 'I wish to see Mr Napier, please—Mr Brent Napier.'

The girl's eyes did not flicker. 'Which company do you represent, madam? I shall know then which member of staff can best help you.'

Linette shook her head with a smile. 'No other person will do. It's Mr Napier I want to see.'

The young woman's expression closed down. 'I'm sorry, but he's not available—unless you have an appointment?'

'I—I don't really need an appointment.' Desperately she pulled at her amethyst ring, transferring it to her engagement finger. 'You see, I'm his fiancée.' She lifted her left hand in a pretence of smoothing her wind-tossed hair.

The woman caught a glimpse of the symbol of betrothal—a glimpse was all Linette wanted her to have. The head of an organisation such as this would buy his wife-to-be a rather more expensive ring than her parents had been able to afford.

Still the young woman frowned. 'That's odd. Hazel, his secretary, would have told me if——' The receptionist smiled. 'Maybe she forgot. Just a minute, I'll talk to her.'

Linette wandered back to join her uncle. He had not moved an inch from where she had left him. The woman beckoned her back. With her hand over the mouthpiece, she said, 'I'm so sorry, I forgot to ask your name.'

'Miss Kemp, Linette Kemp.'

This was repeated into the mouthpiece. There was a pause, then, 'Hazel remembers your name, Miss Kemp.

She said she thought you were Mr Napier's housekeeper.'

Linette coloured deeply, cursing herself for doing so. Remembering well the day Brent's secretary had phoned her at home, Linette shook her head. 'She's mistaken. I'm his fiancée.'

Another softly-spoken discussion took place. With the bustle and noise all around her, Linette could not catch a word. At last the receiver was lowered to its cradle. 'Hazel—Mr Napier's secretary says will you go up and she'll see what she can do to squeeze you in between Mr Napier's appointments.'

Linette nodded and turned, calling imperiously, 'Uncle Godfrey, we're going to see Brent. Which floor did you say?' she asked the receptionist, then immediately realised her mistake. Brent Napier's fiancée would know exactly which floor his suite of offices occupied.

The receptionist began to look anxious, eyeing them both uncertainly. 'Tenth floor, Miss Kemp. The lift is over there.'

As she slipped her hand round her uncle's arm—he would not otherwise have taken a step—she felt the eyes of the young woman fixed on their backs. The entrance foyer seemed endless, each shining floor tile a fateful step towards who knew what humiliation? Brent Napier was quite capable of ejecting her physically if he so desired. Or, she tried to lighten her heart as the lift doors closed on the comings and goings, calling in the bailiffs to do it for him.

The young bellboy, it seemed, knew where they were going. He appeared also to have been programmed by some unseen hand to escort them to the secretary's door. He knocked on it with as much confidence as if he were a top executive himself. Linette envied him his panache. He even opened the door and bowed them in.

'Miss Kemp,' a smiling, slim, browned-haired woman came forward to welcome her, 'I'm Hazel. I'm so sorry about the mix-up. You should have told me. I never dreamt you were Mr Napier's fiancée—— ' She saw Godfrey hovering. 'Oh, you have someone with you.'

'My uncle, Mr Barker,' Linette explained.

'Don't worry about me,' Godfrey growled, and sat in a high-backed chair. He seized a magazine from a low table and opened it at random. Linette bent down to read its name.

'Uncle,' she laughed, 'you don't know anything about pharmaceuticals——' She laughed again, realising why she could read the title so easily. The magazine was upside down in his hands. She removed it and gave him a copy of that day's evening paper.

There were voices from an adjoining room. One was feminine and slightly raised. Godfrey's head came up. A moment later he had disappeared behind the news-sheet.

'Take a seat, Miss Kemp,' Hazel suggested. 'I'll tell Mr Napier you're here.' Picking up the telephone and pressing a button, she did as she had promised.

'Tell her to wait.' The answer came out loud and clear.

'Thank you,' said Linette with as much dignity as she could find, 'I heard what Mr Napier said.'

The communicating door was opened almost immediately. No eager lover came through it, however. 'Linette, my dear,' Mrs Napier's arms went round the slim figure, 'I'm so delighted, I can't tell you! You and Brent—he's giving me a daughter-in-law at last!'

The door was darkened, as was Brent's expression as he witnessed the scene.

'Why, oh, why didn't you tell me, you two? There've been so many rumours about you going round the village . . . May I see the ring?'

Linette put her left hand behind her back.

'Please come in,' Brent invited coolly. 'A drink, Linette?'

A shake of the head was all she could manage. She made as if to move towards him when Mrs Napier asked, looking at the raised newspaper and brown-trousered legs, 'Who is that?'

The figure might have been made of bronze for all the response she received from it. Her voice lowered unbelievingly. 'Godfrey?'

Slowly the newspaper descended and two worried yet
defiant eyes met hers. 'Aileen?' The news-sheets dropped
to the floor. 'Lin made me come. I didn't want to. Lin,
I'm going home now. I'll manage on my own.'

He was at the door when Aileen caught his arm, tugging
him past her son and into the inner office. 'Oh, Godfrey, my
dear, how good of you to come all this way to collect me!' He
was about to protest when her finger silenced him. 'I'm a free
woman, Godfrey. The company can carry on without me.
I've sold all my shares to my son. Isn't that true, Brent?'

Her son nodded. He had put himself behind his desk.
Linette stood, feeling abandoned, by the side of a four-
seater couch.

'Now we've got a little nest-egg, Godfrey,' Mrs Napier
went on, 'I'll sell my big car and buy a smaller one and
you can drive it. I'll give all my jewellery away, since my
daughter Brenda doesn't want it.

'Who will you give it to, Mother?' Brent asked sharply.

'Why, to my daughter-in-law-to-be, who else?'

'But, Mrs Napier——' Linette protested, looking
imploringly at Brent.

'But, Linette?' Brent's voice was as icy as the look in his
eyes.

'We—we aren't——'

'Married yet?' Mrs Napier took her up. 'No matter.
You soon will be.'

Desperately, Linette shook her head. 'Don't give them
to me, please. You see, Brent doesn't trust me.' Her voice
wavered in spite of herself.

'You mean to look after them? Oh, they're just trinkets.'

'*Trinkets*, Mother? Since when have things made of gold
and platinum and diamonds been trinkets?'

'Oh, she can put them in the bank for safe keeping, if
you're so worried about them. Now, come along, Godfrey.
There's a nice little pub not far from here. It's very old. The
customers are friendly and they do a nice line in sandwiches.'

Linette glanced at her uncle. He looked totally bemused.
It was no use trying to comfort him, as she had in the

worst days after her aunt had died. He had to learn to stand on his own two feet now. He had chosen a fine woman as a companion for the rest of his life. She would give him all the help he needed.

' 'Bye, Uncle,' Linette called, standing in the doorway. 'See you at home some time. Don't forget to invite me to the wedding.'

'And us to yours, dear,' Mrs Aileen Napier answered, with a wicked wink. Linette stared after them. Had she known the true situation all the time?

Linette turned from the secretary's room. 'I'm going now,' she stated. 'Mission accomplished. I won't embarrass you any——'

'Who's a sly one, then?' The feline voice came from Brent's own entrance door, and Nita Cutler insinuated herself into the chief executive's office. 'Engaged, are you, Miss Kemp? To the top man himself! However did you do it?' Her slant-eyed gaze found Brent, then swung back to her victim. 'May I see the ring, Miss Kemp?'

Again, Linette put her hand behind her. 'It's just temporary——' she began, but Nita was not to be diverted. She lifted Linette's arm to the front and looked at the ring. Her gaze went again to Brent, quizzical this time.

'Couldn't you do better than that, Brent?' she asked silkily. 'Or did you think your country-girl fiancée wasn't worth better?'

Linette pressed her lips together. Between this man and his mistress she felt like a lamb between two hungry wolves. Verbally, they could—and probably would if she let them—tear her to pieces.

'Linette?' He held out his hand for her left hand. She complied with his wishes. In such a situation there was no alternative. He eyed the ring, eyebrows lifted. 'Yours?'

'A gift from my parents.'

He removed it and slipped it into his pocket, then from the other pocket he extracted another ring. 'My mother's,' he said. 'It was her mother's.' The ring was a circle of diamonds on yellow gold. He slipped it on to her finger.

'Ah,' Nita commented smoothly, 'that's far more suitable for the wife-to-be of Brent Napier. May you long enjoy him, Miss Kemp. That is, what he'll give you of himself—which, as I've discovered, is little indeed.'

Strange, Linette thought, how the bitterness was muted. 'Nita.'

'Yes, Brent?' Her tone was back to normal.

'Now my mother has resigned from the company, your job as her secretary has gone.'

'Your *mother's* secretary?' Linette exclaimed.

Her exclamation was ignored. Brent was saying, 'I'm upgrading you.' Nita waited. 'To be my personal assistant, press liaison, public relations, and so on. Harder work, more money.'

Nita's eyes shone. 'Thanks, Brent.' With a meaningful glance at Linette, she added, 'I'll thank you privately, some time.'

Brent nodded and it was a dismissal. 'Goodbye, Miss Kemp. Congratulations on your catch of the year. You deserve him.' With which enigmatic comment, she withdrew herself from the room.

'Won't you take a seat?' The impersonal invitation made fingers of ice walk down Linette's spine. She shook her head and he shrugged, also remaining standing.

Why did she have to love this man of all men? Linette asked herself in despair. Why did she love the way his hair dipped over his forehead, the roughness of his face when he needed a shave, the sight and feel of his body strength which she had come to know so well?

'I'm sorry I had to resort to false pretences to gain entrance to your presence,' Linette offered, reluctant to apologise.

He flicked her a glance which took in her clothes, her shape, her hair clustering in curls around her neck. 'If you'd said you had come for an interview as an assistant secretary to Hazel, you'd have got past reception.'

'I'm sorry you don't approve of the way I'm dressed.'

'Who said I didn't?' His tone was so detached she wanted

to shake him, to batter him just as she had the day he had stood watching the bailiffs carrying out his orders. He hadn't changed, not one bit, she told herself miserably.

'Anyway, it doesn't matter any more what you think. We can drop the charade.' She eased off the ring he had given her and handed it over. 'Will you please return my ring now?'

He accepted his mother's ring, but made no move to recover hers from his pocket. 'In my own good time,' he answered casually.

'I want it now,' she said through her teeth.

All she received in response was another dismissing look.

'Goodbye, Brent.' She retrieved her bag from the desk.

'Going? Where?'

'Home, the cottage, thank goodness to my own company. But I'm moving as soon as I can find somewhere else.' He continued turning the pages of a catalogue. 'Ever since you first saw me,' she persisted, 'you've wanted to evict me. Well, I'm evicting myself—from your life.'

'Where are you going to live? With Dickins?'

'Leslie? You know his wife's gone back to him.'

'You could always persuade him to buy you a little love-nest. Or couldn't he manage two women?' The look he shot at her held cold contempt. 'I must confess he didn't seem to me to have the strength for one, let alone two.'

Linette gripped her bag. 'I hate you, Brent Napier!'

'I've heard that before,' he responded indifferently. The phone rang, and he picked up the receiver and listened. 'Put him through, will you?'

He nodded to Linette, his mind apparently and entirely on his work. He was dismissing her as if she were an employee! There was nothing she could do in such a situation to salvage her self-respect. But tomorrow, she vowed, when she started looking for a room somewhere, she would find herself again.

It was late when she arrived back home, but not so late that the telephone didn't ring. Her heart had not lifted, thinking it could be Brent, so she was not disappointed when Leslie spoke.

'Linette? You're back at last! I've been trying all evening. I just wanted to tell you,' he had to swallow before he could continue, 'that Jane and I are together again. Jenny just can't believe her mummy's come back.'

I'll bet you can't either, Linette thought. 'I'm so happy for you, both of you,' she told him, sounding pleased without much difficulty, since she was pleased.

'We—Jane and I—would like to thank you for everything you've done, Lin. And Jane says she's sorry, really sorry, about what she said to you last night. If only she'd known you were engaged, and to Mr Napier, she would have believed you straight away. Sorry I let you down, Linette, by implicating you, but——'

'You were so busy hurting each other,' Linette interrupted, 'you didn't care who else you might be hurting. I know, Leslie, and I forgive you.' But only just, she thought. If you hadn't lied, Jane wouldn't have come storming round here, and Brent wouldn't have overheard and—oh, so many things wouldn't have happened.

'Jenny sends her love,' Leslie finished. 'Goodbye, Lin. And congratulations, from both of us.'

Linette sat down, clasping her hands and trying to smile away the threatening tears. That's two couples happy, she told herself, Uncle Godfrey and his Aileen, Leslie and his runaway wife. Who's left? She shook her head, refusing to pursue the subject.

Tired though she was, Linette could not relax sufficiently to sleep. The cold, impassive face of the man behind the desk in that large room, with its array of armchairs and couches, its modern paintings on fabric-lined walls, kept looming out of the darkness to taunt her staring eyes.

In desperation, she switched on the small lamp and sat hugging her knees. Maybe a hot drink would calm her down, she reasoned, knowing in her heart that nothing could do that now. The parting of the ways between herself and Brent Napier had come at last. It was something she would have to face and eventually accept.

If a lifetime of married happiness such as her parents

enjoyed was not to be hers, then she would have to accept that, too. No one else would ever take the place of the man with whom she had fallen in love. Maybe, she sighed, pushing aside the covers, she'd find a man one day, a good man to whom she could give her deep affection. Although it wouldn't be love . . .

As she drank the weak tea she had made for herself, there came the sound of the key in the door. Clutching the mug between stiff fingers, she found herself holding her breath. Brent was back, he had come home! Her legs twined tautly together as she perched on the high stool.

He came into the kitchen, removing his tie and shedding his jacket which he hung on the back of the door. Then he looked at her long and hard. 'You're still here, then?' The sarcasm was unmistakable.

'Tomorrow,' she told him, her voice firm with false courage, 'tomorrow I'll start looking for somewhere.'

He went without answering, to his jacket pocket. 'Your ring.' She accepted it and pushed it on to her right hand. 'My mother's ring to be returned to her.' He placed it on a shelf of the wooden dresser. He raked in the other pocket and withdrew a velvet-covered box.

Eyes staring, Linette watched as he flicked open the lid. A solitaire diamond ring sparkled from its interior. Brent pulled the ring from the box and walked over to her. He removed her empty mug, then took her left hand in his, slipping the ring on to her engagement finger.

'Diamond and platinum. Is it comfortable? I took the size from your own ring.'

'Exactly right,' she whispered. With admiration for its perfection, she gazed at it. 'Who is it for?'

He clicked the box shut, pushing it into his trouser pocket. 'For you, and you damned well knew it!'

'I didn't, I swear I didn't. It's an engagement ring, and I'm not engaged to anyone. Don't say it's you, because you wouldn't marry me if I was the only woman alive. That's what you said.'

'I take back those words. Will you marry me?'

'No, I won't marry you. Thank you,' she added with a politeness that seemed to amuse him. He took his amusement with him up the stairs, each step sounding heavy on the wooden treads. He was a tired man. What a welcome she had given him! And he had just presented her with a very expensive diamond ring.

He was playing with her, she justified her cool reception of him, tantalising her when she knew he had put up permanent barriers to her ever becoming his wife. Gazing at the ring, she grew puzzled.

Lifting her trailing dressing-gown from the floor, she hurried after him. He was in the bathroom, stripped to the waist. He must have heard her coming, yet he did not turn as she stood in the doorway. His fingers were rubbing over his jaw as he looked in the cabinet mirror.

'Why did you ask me to marry you?' she demanded.

Brent turned now, an eyebrow raised. 'Those rumours everyone keeps telling us about—it was the gentlemanly thing to do, wasn't it?'

'Why should you worry about village gossip, a man in your powerful position in the world? Or maybe,' she added, too sweetly, 'you had my interests at heart?'

Another mocking look came her way. He put the plug in the washbasin and ran the water. His broad expanse of back with its ripple of muscles as he moved tormented her senses until her fists clenched and she had to push them into her dressing-gown pockets.

'I don't care about rumours,' she informed him, watching as he washed his face. 'I'm leaving the district, so they don't worry me.'

'Give me your address,' he muttered, sluicing his face. 'I'll need it when I call to collect you for our wedding ceremony.'

An exasperated sigh escaped her. 'I'm not going to marry you!' she almost shouted. 'I'm tainted, remember? You said that, too. You wouldn't want to follow another man in—in making love to me.'

He was drying his face and paused, holding the towel

about his cheeks so that only his eyes showed. It annoyed her that she couldn't see whether he was laughing at her or condemning her.

With an irritable expelling of her breath, she said, 'Good night,' and closed her door. It was only when she had settled into bed that she realised she was still wearing Brent's ring. Tomorrow, she thought sleepily, I'll return it to him. Her fingers felt for it. Just for tonight, she would love it as she loved him.

In a sleepy haze, her eyes fluttered open. The door was creaking, a man was coming in. He was dressed in a towelling robe. His large, menacing outline disappeared, giving place to substance as he mercilessly switched on the light.

'Brent?' She pushed the hair from her eyes, blinking in the brightness. 'What do you want?'

He did not speak, but pulled back the clothes and scooped her into his arms. 'I'm not——' she cried, 'I won't—you can't make me!' But she knew he could and he would. If he did, she would belong to him in every sense of the word.

'The ring, the proposal of marriage,' she persisted as he carried her, 'they're just a means to an end. A way you've found of getting what you want from me, and making it seem moral and right.'

He dropped her on to his bed, but she swung her legs round as she had done the last time. He had let her go then, and he would have to, again. 'You will not make me into one of your women!'

Her stormy face gazed up at him, finding in his eyes a resolution so strong she knew she didn't stand a chance against him. His robe was pulled open to the tie-belt and her eyes were caught by the expanse of chest she had come to know so well. His hair was over his forehead and it was plain that he had decided not to shave.

Still he said nothing. Linette was nonplussed by his silence. Somehow she would make him speak! She kicked out towards him with her bare feet, but he merely bent to hold her legs still, then while his robe stayed closed below the waist, he trapped her legs between the bareness of his.

The feel of his rough-textured thighs against her own smooth-skinned limbs was electric. He slipped the straps of her nightdress from her shoulders, pulling it to her waist.

Discarding his robe at last, he stood over her, arms folded, and she knew he had nearly won. The sight of him standing there, so powerful, his physique so lean and strong, made her mouth go dry. Her pulses hammered with a longing for him that superseded all the other times she had wanted him to touch her. Slowly he moved her covering arms from her breasts.

'Brent, oh, Brent, I——'

It was enough for him. It brought him down, swinging her legs with his own on to the bed. He discarded her nightdress completely, throwing it across the room. His lips trailed a line from her throat to her breasts, savouring to the full the sweetness he found there. In her joy at his possession of the hardening rosy tips, she cried out that she loved him.

Her fingers caught up in his hair, moved clutchingly to the muscles of his shoulders. Her head turned from side to side as his hands found her stomach, stroking it, then trailing to intimate places.

His eyes, as they captured her pleasure-crazed look, burned with a blazing male desire. 'Now will you marry me?' he asked, his tone harsh with demand for an immediate answer.

Linette closed her eyes to blot out the face that had been tormenting her almost from the first time she saw him. 'You don't mean it. It's payment you're taking now. You said one day you would. And—and you think I'm any man's woman——'

'*Will you give me an answer!*' Tears started and he saw them and reached with his lips to kiss them away. 'I love you, Linette, do you hear? I need you—in my bed, in my life, by my side. Now will you marry me?'

'I'll marry you, Brent,' she answered breathlessly. 'I've wanted nothing else since the first moment I saw you.'

'At last you're telling me what I want to hear. I'm going to take you, do you understand? There's no going back now.'

There was no mistaking his clamouring needs, the compelling, pulsing strength of his passion. His thumb went on making rough circles around her breasts, teasing and moulding and making her ache for the fulfilment of his lovemaking. He took her at last, and his gentleness brought tears of thankfulness and joy.

Later, when reluctantly they drew apart, they lay entwined, her hair spread over his chest against which her cheek lay. She listened as his pounding heart slowed to its normal steady pace.

As she sat up to pull the covers over them, Brent demanded roughly, 'Where are you going?'

'Just keeping out the cold, darling,' she teased.

'You're staying until morning. Understand?'

'Yes, Brent.' She snuggled against him and his arms enfolded her. 'I'll stay all the rest of my life, if you want.'

'Our lives,' he corrected her. 'Come closer, sweetheart.' He moved her until they were entangled.

'What made you change your mind about me?' she asked, running a finger over his lips.

He looked down at her quizzically. 'Investigation, via the telephone after you'd left my office. I called the Dickins residence, and he corroborated your story. He said the next-door neighbour would tell me the truth if I didn't believe him. He said how sorry he was for involving you in his family quarrel, but thanked you, too, for letting him see how much his wife had really cared.'

'When we're married, Brent,' she smoothed her hand down his arm, bumping over the muscles, 'will you go on seeing Nita?'

'Every day.' He felt her stiffen against him and he pulled her closer, running his palm over her hip and thigh. 'You heard me tell her about her promotion.'

With her hands she pushed herself from him, tugging at his ring on her finger. 'You can have this back—I won't be marrying you after all.'

Brent pushed the ring back and held it there. 'Jealous?'

He tipped her face to his. 'I can see you are. It's what I intended. Nita was a good actress.'

Linette frowned. 'You mean that when she came here——'

'We talked business. She couldn't speak to my mother. You know why, don't you?' She nodded. 'So she gave me messages, showed me letters to be signed, files to be looked through.' He put his lips against her ear. 'We did nothing else, nothing at all. Which is why, quite fortuitously, you tripped over me the other night while I slept on the floor.'

'So it was all pretence, to make me jealous?' Her fist began to pound his chest, light blows that he hardly felt. He caught her wrist and smiled.

'This, my darling, is where we came in, as they say. The day you used me as a punchball, I decided I would have you for my wife.'

'Your own mother said that you'd stop at nothing to get your own way.'

'Now you know she was right. You first took my fancy,' she made as if to bite his shoulder but he caught her mouth with a kiss, 'the first time I ever saw you, behind that fruit and flower stall.'

'Yet you actually did your best to evict us!'

'I didn't, did I? Anyway, I had this cottage lined up for you and your uncle, but I was damned if I was going to tell you that while you were trying to batter me senseless.'

'You were a monster, Brent, to do what you did.' Her arms reached up to curl round his neck. 'But not any more. You're the most wonderful——'

'And you're the most beautiful woman a man could ever have for a wife. Three days from tomorrow, we shall be married. Until then . . .'

He pushed her on to her back and covered her mouth with his. She felt the desire in him increase, stirring hers to returning life. 'I want you now,' he whispered against her mouth. 'For as long as we live, I'll never stop wanting you.'

'And for the rest of our lives, I'll never stop giving,' she whispered back, as he gathered her into his arms.

# ROMANCE

## Mills & Boon Reader Film Service

### See your pictures before you pay

Our confidence in the quality of our colour prints is
such that we send the developed film to you
without asking for payment in advance. We bill
you for only the prints that you receive, which
means that if your prints don't come out, you won't
just be sent an annoying credit note as with the
'cash with order' film services.

### Free Kodacolor Film

We replace each film sent for processing with a
fresh Kodacolor film to fit the customer's camera
without further charge. Kodak's suggested prices in
the shops are:

110/24 exp. £1.79
126/24 exp. £1.88
135/24 exp. £1.88
135/36 exp. £2.39

### Top Quality Colour Prints

We have arranged for your films to be developed by
the largest and longest established firm of mail
order film processors in Britain. We are confident
that you will be delighted with the quality they
produce. Our commitment, and their technical
expertise ensures that we stay ahead.

### How long does it take?

Your film will be in their laboratory for a maximum
of 48 hours. We won't deny that problems can
occasionally arise or that the odd film requires

# Mills & Boon Reader Film Service

special attention resulting in a short delay.
Obviously the postal time must be added and we
cannot eliminate the possibility of an occasional
delay here but your film should take no longer than
7 days door-to-door.

## What you get

Superprints giving 30% more picture area than the
old style standard enprint. Print sizes as follows:

| Print Size | from 35mm | from 110 | from 126 |
|---|---|---|---|
| Superprints | $4'' \times 5\frac{3}{4}''$ | $4'' \times 5\frac{1}{8}''$ | $4'' \times 4''$ |

All sizes approximate.
All prints are borderless, have round corners and a
sheen surface.

## Prices

No developing charge, you only pay for each
successful print:
Superprints   22p each.
This includes VAT at the current rate and applies to
100 ASA film only. Prices apply to UK only. There is
no minimum charge.
We handle colour negative film for prints only and
Superprints can only be made from 35mm, 126 and
110 film which is for C41 process.

If you have any queries 'phone 0734 597332 or
write to: Customer Service, Mills & Boon Reader
Film Service, P.O. Box 180, Reading RG1 3PF.